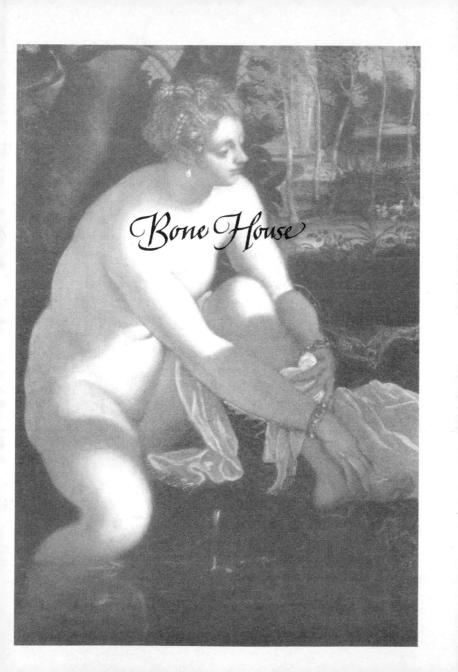

Bone House

Bone House

Betsy Tobin

review

First published 2000
by REVIEW

An imprint of Headline Book Publishing

10 9 8 7 6 5 4 3 2 1

British Library Cataloguing in Publication Data

Tobin, Betsy
Bone House
I.Title
823.9'14[F]

ISBN 0 7472 7225 5

Typeset by Letterpart Ltd
Reigate, Surrey

Printed and bound in Great Britain by
Clays Ltd, St Ives plc.

HEADLINE BOOK PUBLISHING
A division of the Hodder Headline Group
338 Euston Road
London NW1 3BH

www.headline.co.uk
www.hodderheadline.com

For Peter

For our small body is the microcosm:
it understands what is seen in air, on earth, at sea . . .

Francois Du Port, 1694
A Decade Of Medicine: The Physician Of The Rich And Poor

Chapter One

Her death has made us numb. Dora, the great-bellied woman, lies frozen in the ground. And like some part we've lost to frostbite, our minds still reach for her. The men of the village wear a wandering look in their eyes. They forget their work, leave their tools lying idle, drink to excess, then roam like dogs until they drop in the mud. Even the women are uneasy, for though she was one of us, we could never hope to fill her shoes. The great-bellied woman, with her door-wide hips and plate-sized breasts, was more woman than we could ever be. We even envied her belly: her great, laden belly, filled with the fruits of her whoring.

She left behind the boy, the giant boy, her only child. He is built like an ox, just as she was, though he is slow of speech, and some say also of thought. But this is unfair for he is not yet a man, but a boy of eleven trapped in a man's body. She christened him Johann, a name from her past, but from the beginning she called him Long Boy. Yesterday, when she was laid

1

to ground, Long Boy trembled and nearly broke with grief. He collapsed, sobbing like a child, but it took four strong men to carry him home. I do not know what will become of him now that she is gone. And neither do I know what will become of us, for some people are the centre of their world, and others are the spokes.

She came across the water, blown like a seed, and touched down here. In the beginning there was talk she'd killed a man across the sea, though she never spoke of it and no one dared ask her, no more than they would ask the Queen. But if she did he was probably deserving. Dora lived by her own rules, but they were not unjust. I admired her for this: she was not bound by superstition, nor by fear, nor by other people's prejudice. She did not justify herself to anyone, no more than she sought the whys and wherefores of those who pitched up on her doorstep. These were mostly men, but women came as well, for different reasons. She gave counsel freely, offered food and shelter, and sometimes even money to those who needed it. But mostly she gave of herself, her big, bounteous self, and those who sought her bed paid handsomely for it.

Her death was sudden, a freakish accident. They found her frozen, her belly to the sky, at the bottom of a ravine. She'd taken a short cut through the forest and had slipped on snow-covered rocks which were slick with ice underneath. She would not have died except for a blow to the back of her head from a sharp stone which edged the stream. She'd clearly tried to stop herself; in her death-grip was a sapling torn from the banks as she fell. But with her great weight, it would have done little to slow her. Her feet sliced through a pool of ice at the bottom, and it held her fast up to the thighs. In the end it was the chisel that set her free. Her blood was everywhere, they said.

I saw it later, a dirty spray of ink across the snow.

I was five when she first came to the village. She was great-bellied even then, but she carried her burden easily, not in an ungainly way as so many of the village women do. One day at market I was scrambling in the dirt while my mother haggled over the price of carp. Thinking I would hide, I crawled under the fishwife's cart. At length I heard my mother calling me, her voice impatient. I did not go at first, but kept my place and listened to her calling. I remember hearing her voice climb and swell, like birdsong when it builds at dusk. It made my pulse race as it became more shrill; the sound of her fear pleased me. But when she finally screamed my name my stomach lurched, and I scrambled out from under the cart, only to collide head first with Dora's rock-hard abdomen.

She did not even flinch, but reached down and lifted me high. And as I scaled the heights of her body, I found myself staring straight into her eyes, pale blue, with speckled flecks of brown, like pigeon eggs. She said not a word, only handed me to my mother, whose face by now was tight with fear. My mother gave a brief nod of thanks and took me from her, squeezing me so hard that I burst into tears. Then Dora laid her own hand gently on my mother's arm, and in an instant I saw the fear and anger ebb from my mother's eyes, as if Dora had siphoned it away through her outstretched fingers. Suddenly I felt my mother's grip release. I stopped crying and we stood, the three of us, for a moment. Then Dora let go of my mother's arm.

'They say you are a midwife,' she addressed us haltingly. My mother nodded, her eyes dipping for an instant to the woman's swollen belly. 'I am in need of you,' she continued. Her voice was low and thick, and her accent strange. She spoke slowly and with care, as if plucking fruit from a tree. My mother nodded, her own voice failing her at first.

'Come to me at dusk,' she said finally. Then Dora smiled and turned away, and I watched her disappear with long strides through the market crowds.

When she came to us that evening I was already in bed, but I watched from behind the curtain as my mother kneeled in front of her and spanned her belly with her hands. I saw her chest rise and fall and heard the sound of her breathing, hard and regular, like a horse's. The air was heavy as my mother worked her hands around the globe of her abdomen, turning her palms at different angles, pressing and probing, then smoothing the taut skin beneath them. She leaned forward and pressed an ear to Dora's belly, her outstretched hands resting gently on each side of the sphere. At length she rocked back on her heels.

'It will be soon,' she said.

Dora nodded.

'This is not the first,' my mother ventured, looking up at her.

'No.'

'The others?' she asked cautiously. Dora gave a brief shake of her head. My mother acknowledged this with a circumspect nod. If she taught me one thing as a child, it was the importance of discretion where women's secrets were concerned.

'You will be staying in the village?' asked my mother.

'Yes,' she replied decisively. 'Here I will live.'

Dora moved into the miller's cottage. He had died of cholera only weeks before, as had his wife and only son before him, and the cottage remained empty. She cleared it out, burning his furniture and woollens in a huge pyre of flames, a gesture of extravagance that many thought unnecessary. She then proceeded to make her own, hauling timber herself from the forest. She had arrived on horseback laden with her belongings, and within a few weeks she had sold the horse and built or purchased the few remaining things she needed. It was clear from the beginning that she had come to stay, and after a short time no one questioned her presence.

I do not know when she began to trade her body, or how it happened, or indeed whether she had planned it so. Only that it seemed both right and natural. As a child I used to play outside her cottage. Men came and went, and always they were cheerful. When I asked my mother why Dora had so many visitors, she told me that the house was a shop, selling things that people liked but did not need. This I took to mean food, and for a time I imagined a secret cellar full of rare delicacies and sweetmeats. But when I asked whether we could not taste the things she had for sale, my mother said they would not appeal to us. To me this meant food from the sea: oysters, cockles, jellied eel and the like, which I have always disliked. When I asked my mother whether this was the type of fare Dora served, she paused and said it was much the same. So I came to think of her house as a sort of tavern, where men could come and gorge like kings, and feel contented.

Later, when I was old enough to know the truth, I wondered at my mother's explanation, for it seemed to me that the men who crossed her doorstep did so as much out of need as desire. For life was often hard, and there was little enough to relieve it. In winter there was famine and sickness and bitter cold to contend with. In summer, there was fever and pestilence. When I was five nearly half the village succumbed to plague. My mother did not let me out of the house for weeks on end, and I remember watching through the cracks of the doorway as the bodies were taken away on horse carts to be burned in fields outside the village.

Throughout my childhood Dora plied her trade, entertaining both the men of the village and those passing through on the road to London. It dawned on me eventually that my mother did not have such a need, for as long as I could remember she preferred her own company to that of others. She was not reclusive, only purposeful; when she did keep company, it was with women, and these were usually great-bellied. Her work was her life, and even I felt incidental to it at times. My grandmother had birthed children, and her mother before that, and as far as I knew my own mother had done nothing but reach into wombs since she had come of age. That she'd once been a child herself seemed unlikely; that she'd actually conceived one was unthinkable.

But this was not the case with most of the village. As soon as I was old enough to understand, I kept track of those who visited Dora's house. I have a good memory for a face, and an even better one for a voice, and a great deal could be heard through the cottage walls. At one time or another, every able-bodied man in the village came her way, as did a sizeable proportion of those who were not so abled. She did not discriminate but welcomed all of them with an easy smile and a ready hand. And as I have said, the women came as well, their baskets full of new-picked apples and just-baked bread. They came less often, but to me their need seemed just as great. They were drawn not by lust but by the desire for her presence. For with her grace and generosity and compassion, she transformed us; the simple fact that she had chosen us filled us with pride. And for me at least, there was something else gained by her presence: a glimpse of what lay beyond our small horizons.

That is why we are now stricken by her death. Even my mother is bereft. Perhaps especially my mother, for Dora was the closest thing she ever had to a friend. Yesterday, during the funeral procession, my mother stumbled on some loose stones and nearly fell. She pitched forward suddenly, grabbing my arm for support, and for an instant I was reminded of the moment we first met Dora. My mother again gripped me so hard I nearly cried out, though she appeared not to realise it. But this time, there was no one there to carry off her anger, nor her loss. My mother clutched my arm all the way to the grave site, so hard it later brought blood marks to my skin, but still it did not raise Dora from her grave.

After the funeral, I took my mother home and put her to bed. These past few months age has made its mark upon her, a process only hastened by the events of the last three days. I heated some broth for her to eat but she refused, sinking down into her bed with a raspy breath. My mother has been a party to death more times than I could number (in some years, more babies are born still than live), but she has always distanced herself from its impact. Yesterday, it seemed as if all those deaths had finally caught up to her, and that she could not bear the weight of them another second. I built up the fire and sat in front of it until I thought she was asleep, but when I left I was not certain, for her face was to the wall.

Then I went to see Long Boy. When I arrived at Dora's cottage, I found him crouched in front of the fire wrapped in blankets. His eyes, large and round like his mother's, were swollen from crying, and his tangled mass of dark hair stood on end. In his hand was a loaf of bread, and on the table more loaves were piled of various shapes and sizes, together with plates of meat, gifts from the women of the village. His appetite was legendary; his mother often joked that he was the only male in the village whose hunger she could not satisfy. He took great bites of bread, chewing rhythmically, absently, his eyes glued to the fire. The act of eating seemed to calm him.

I was surprised to find him alone. What had become of the four men who returned with him? I wondered. And the others, the ones with plates of food? Where were *they*, now that she was dead? The cottage had been emptied not just of her, but of all of them, for I sensed that they could no more tolerate his presence than do without hers. He was a strange child, unlike other children; he would appear from nowhere, and disappear just as suddenly. He rarely spoke, and when he did, it was to ask a question, often an unsettling one. When I entered the cottage he looked up at me for an instant, then turned back to the fire. He was accustomed to seeing outsiders enter his home. I laid my things on the table with the others: some hard-cooked eggs, a knuckle of bacon, a lump of butter. I drew up the only other chair in the cottage, and sat down next to him. He bit off another huge bite of bread from the loaf in his hand, his jaw working hard up and down, the cords of his long neck bulging as he swallowed. I sat with him for several minutes, and when he'd finished the bread, he stared down at his empty hands.

'Johann,' I said, leaning forward. He did not respond, so I waited a moment, then tried again. 'Long Boy.' He looked up at me and blinked, rubbing his face with the palms of his hands, then his eyes wandered towards the pile of food on the table. 'What will you do?' I asked.

He reached for another piece of bread.

'Will you stay here? By yourself?' I said.

'Who will stay with me?' he asked.

I looked at him a moment, then shook my head. 'There is no one,' I said. 'But there are places you could go. You could find work. You're nearly grown.' My words were ridiculous: he was almost twice my size.

He shook his head and took another bite of bread. We sat for a few minutes in silence. He continued to eat, and only when he was finished did he turn to me, his eyes blurry with confusion.

'Why did she fall?'

I looked at him and hesitated. Why indeed, with all her strength and grace and spirit, why would she succumb so easily to death? I closed my eyes and in an instant she appeared, shaking free her lion's head of nut-brown hair. When I opened my eyes, Long Boy was staring at me, mouth wide with waiting.

'I do not know,' was all I said.

Chapter Two

I stayed with him until he slept, curled like a cat, in front of the fire. Then I set out for the Great House, traversing the length of the village with its dishevelled row of farmer's cottages. The Great House sits atop a small hillock on the outskirts of the village. Its grounds are neatly marked out by a low stone wall which I used to straddle as a child, my eyes trained on the house's imposing façade for signs of life within. To the rear of the house are formal gardens, which descend in graceful arcs until the ground levels out in a sort of boggy meadow, ending in a small stream which often overflows in spring. To the right of the house are the outbuildings, including a small stone chapel which is built into the hillside; to the left is an orchard of apple and pear and elderflower.

The Great House never fails to soothe me. I have always felt upon entering it that I could leave myself at the door, place it on a hook with the hats and scarves, and once inside I am lost behind the screens to other people's lives. It is a useful refuge. It is also my livelihood, and my abode. I left my mother's house five years ago, when it became clear that we could no longer live together under one roof.

When I first came to the Great House it was to assist in the kitchen, making bread and scrubbing vegetables. My mistress took a liking to me and within a short time I was made her chambermaid, sleeping on a trundle bed outside her chambers, and scurrying about in the night to satisfy her nocturnal whims, which were many. It was she who taught me to read and write, as my mother had been unable because she herself could barely sign her name. I was given daily lessons, together with readings of the Scriptures, for the first few years; now it is I who read to her, for she is decrepit and her eyes are failing. For a while she taught two other girls as well, my replacement in the kitchens, and the laundry maid, but neither showed a facility for learning and they were eventually left to Cook's devices. They and Cook and I are the only women in the house, aside from my mistress. With the exception of Josiah, my master's private steward, the manservants come and go; there is little opportunity for them to rise here, as the estate is not grand enough. A few have stayed but some have left to seek their fortunes elsewhere. In all we number twelve or thirteen. We take our meals together in the great hall, while the master and his mother, my mistress, dine in privacy in the adjoining chamber.

To sit at table with so many was a novelty for me at first; always it had been just my mother and I, alone with our silence for company. In the beginning I found the coarse talk of the men and table banter of the girls alarming; early on I found it difficult to eat at all, so much so that my weight dwindled to that of a stable boy. Eventually I mastered my senses and could speak my mind, though I still found the bawdy humour and sly insinuations not to my taste. I suppose I am my mother's daughter in that respect, for she has little time and even less facility for an exchange of wit. Her words are full of truth but empty of grace or subtlety; it is the latter which my mistress has tried to cultivate in me. Perhaps I am the daughter she never had, though I have never felt affection for her, only loyalty. For this I am amply rewarded. I now have my own bedchamber at the top of the house; not big but private, with a small rectangular window tucked under the eave. Inside, there is a real mattress and pillow, with bleached linen sheets to sleep on, and a rough-hewn trunk to hold my few possessions, most of which are gifts from her. Every year at Christmas she makes a present of some cloth which I make up into a dress or cape. The first year I cut it carefully so there would be extra left to make a bonnet for my mother. When I gave it to her she pursed her lips and thanked me, but I have never seen her wear it.

It is the windows of the Great House I prize above all. I love the way the sunlight passes through the leaded glass, creating patterns on the floor that vanish in an instant, like a whim. Before I came to the Great House, I lived in near-darkness. My mother's house had only one window, open to the elements and facing to the north. The sun did not shine through it, and the house was always cold as a result. We lived in one room and shared a bed, which was large and hung with curtains all round to keep out the draught. The cottage was one of several rented from my master; we were the only tenants in the row who did not farm. To a greater or lesser extent our fortune still depended on the harvest; in famine years, there were fewer babies to be born, and little money to pay my mother's fees. But in times of plenty, we did well. My mother had a reputation that extended far beyond the village. She often travelled to neighbouring towns, and once attended royalty who were passing through en route to London. The baby was born early and died, but my mother was still rewarded with more gold sovereigns than we had ever seen, as she had acted quickly and saved the mother's life.

I was fourteen when I took up residence at the Great House. I was small for my age and had not yet a woman's body. Cook took one look at me and laughed, saying I was not large enough to stew, let alone to help prepare one. But I worked harder than the others and kept my tongue, and soon I'd earned my place. There are advantages that come with being slight: I move about the house more freely than the others, and as a consequence am privy to its secrets. It is a large house, built by my master's grandfather in the style of his time, but it has been added to by both succeeding generations. The result is a hotchpotch of

function and design. My master's father added wings
to the north and west; the former houses utility
rooms and servants' quarters, the latter a sumptuous
guest chamber, fit for nobility, which is rarely put to
use. My own master added a massive hexagonal turret
to the east, with a library on the ground floor and a
circular stairway leading to a gabled tower. At the very
top is a viewing platform which only he makes use of.
The turret gives the house a slightly lopsided appearance overall, being out of proportion to the rest, and
oddly placed. My master himself is misshapen, his
spine bent like a hook from an accident at birth, and I
have often felt that he built the tower in his own
image, so he would feel more at home. For the Great
House is very much my master's hearth: he does not
move easily among those of his class, and rarely
ventures forth from his own grounds.

He is the antithesis of his mother, my mistress, who
longs to keep company with others, despite her age
and failing health. Her husband died when I was but a
child, and since then she has struggled to maintain her
place in what little society our county affords. She
delights in entertainments of any sort, and follows the
fashions of the Court in London as best she can, which
is ludicrous given her age and relative isolation. There
is a small scattering of minor nobility in the neighbouring parishes with whom she socialises; otherwise
she surrounds herself with physicians and servants,
and in this way generates her own diversions. She is
scrupulous in maintaining her outward appearance

and dress, and my primary task these past few years has been to attend her in such matters – that is, when she does not take to her bed with illness, as she is wont to do when there is little else to distract her. At these times, I am kept busy with frequent applications of salves and ointments, and with Scripture readings, which she believes is beneficial to one's health. All in all, it is relatively easy labour, so much so that my position sometimes causes jealousy within the Great House, though I doubt the others would find her constant advice and tuition easy on their ears. But I have learned to tolerate it, and have developed a facility for listening without hearing, and of maintaining my own private thoughts while reading aloud.

This morning she has taken to her bed, deciding she is ill, and has called upon me to send for her physician. He lives some miles away, and after dispatching one of the stable hands by horse to retrieve him, I return to her bedchamber. When I enter, she is dozing in her bed, and it strikes me that she, like my mother, appears newly aged. Like the Queen she wears a wig in public, and without it her head seems too small, her silver hair so thin it barely shields her scalp. The skin of her face has been ravaged by years of make-up, and it appears rough and reddened when she does not conceal it with powder. She has lost many teeth, giving her mouth a sunken appearance, especially in sleep, and the skin on her neck hangs in great wrinkles. When I enter her chamber, she stirs and opens her eyes for a second, then closes them again and sighs. I seat myself beside her window in my favourite spot and take up my embroidery. She prefers that I attend her even while she sleeps, and I spend many an hour by the window with only my needles and musings for company. At such times I often grow restless, but today I do not care, for my mind is once again occupied by Long Boy.

It now seems strange that only he has questioned his mother's death. She was found by a farmer whose sheep had strayed from their enclosure. It was he who first tried to move her frozen body from the ice. When he could not, he returned to the village and a party of yeoman returned to the scene of the accident. It took them some time to carry her home; in the end they dragged her on a sledge across the icy fields. They laid her out in her cottage, and afterwards I overheard one say that Long Boy had been struck dumb by the sight of her. My mother helped prepare her body for the grave. She said afterwards that the back of Dora's skull had been split open by the sharp stone, and that the blood had flown so freely there was none left remaining. In the few days that followed before she was buried, her house was the scene of much mourning. Every member of the parish came to pay their last respects, and many came from neighbouring villages and towns. While I was there, my mistress's physician came, and I watched as he examined the wound to her head. He raised her eyelids and peered at her pupils, then passed his hands loosely over her limbs and belly in a gesture that struck me as

19

part exploratory, part caress. Finally, he picked up her hands and examined the palms, cradling her long fingers for a moment in his own. He then replaced them and turned away, making for the door. I moved to intercept him, but before I had a chance to speak, he disappeared.

My mistress stirs and raises herself on one elbow, beginning to cough. I move quickly to her side and support her thin frame with my arms. The bones of her shoulders feel like bird bones, as if they will snap under too much pressure. Her brittle frame shakes from the cough, a dry, rasping sound which slices through the stillness of the chamber. When the cough subsides she remains bent over, her breath a whistle, and I stare down at the bald patch at the back of her head, the size of an orange, like babies have. Finally she swallows and raises her head, fixing me with her watery grey eyes.

'I shall perish from this wretched cough,' she says.

'No, mum,' I reply. I hand her a mug of ale, which she takes with a nod. She likes it warm, and drinks copious amounts throughout the day. She slurps down half the liquid in one long draught and hands me the remainder, waving it away.

'Where is Lucius?' she asks.

'On his way, mum.'

'He should live closer,' she says. 'What if I should suffer a stroke?'

'My Lord Carrington is near to hand.'

'I should still perish,' she says with a sniff. 'One cadaver treating another.' This last is not an understatement: her other physician Carrington is so aged he cannot walk without assistance from a manservant. The last time he attended her, he himself was so overcome during the examination that he had to be carried from the room.

I return to my seat by the window, take up my needle and thread. Her eyes trail past me to the glass. Outside the sky is flinty grey and a thick frost covers the stubble in the fields. The winter has been exceptionally harsh, like those I remember from my childhood. She shivers and draws her gown more closely around her shoulders, then lies back against the cushions.

'She must have frozen within the hour,' she says obliquely. It takes me a moment to realise she refers to Dora. 'For her sake at least, I hope that she was already dead,' she continues, her tone not quite indifferent. It is not the first indication I have seen of her disapproval.

'They said she was killed outright by the fall,' I reply.

My mistress raises her eyebrows. 'Perhaps,' she says a little distractedly. 'Perhaps it was the fall after all.'

Something in her tone catches me. I raise my eyes and she is picking at a loose thread on her bedclothes. I frown, hesitate a moment.

'It shattered her skull,' I say. 'Lucius examined her.'

'Many, many times, I should think, over the course

of a lifetime,' she remarks. It occurs to me for the first time that age does not preclude jealousy. I do not look at her, as I can think of nothing to respond that does not smack of disrespect. We sit for a while, with only my needle pricking the silence.

'It is difficult to believe that she is dead,' she says finally. I raise my head and she is looking past me into the greyness, her expression frozen. She turns to me slowly and blinks.

I stare at her, unable to reply.

Lucius arrives an hour later, delayed by the roads, which are barely passable this winter. He bustles in carrying his case of instruments, and clears his throat with measured self-importance. My mistress appears not to notice his affectations. Indeed, she becomes coy whenever he is present, if such a thing is possible for one so old. It is difficult for me to comprehend why she behaves this way. Lucius is not much younger than she, though he is stouter and more robust. His face is not handsome but I suppose his bearing is impressive. His best feature is his hair which, although greying, is thick and lively and entirely his own. Indeed, on a windy day it operates independently of him, and I have often glimpsed him struggling to restrain it outside my mistress's chamber. His eyes are small and pig-like, however, and his nose is prone to redness. Both are made worse by the complete absence of a chin, which he tries to mask with a thin goatee and an oversized ruff.

Still, she flirts with him like a young maid, and sends for him when there is only the slightest provocation. This morning she sits up when he enters, and I am reminded of a bird opening its plume. My mistress has the ability to transform herself at will, to shrug off both age and infirmity when an opportunity presents itself. Lucius is just such a one. He bows to her and she extends a bony hand, which he presses lightly to his lips.

'Your humble servant, madam,' he says.

'You are neither, Lucius,' she responds with a wave. 'But you are nevertheless welcome. I am near death this morning.'

'My lady exaggerates,' he says, stepping forward. 'A touch of colic, nothing more, I should venture.' He picks up her wrist and feels her pulse.

'Perhaps,' she says with a shrug.

He opens his case and takes out a cone-shaped instrument, not unlike the one my mother uses. He motions for her to bend forward and he places it against her back, lowering his ear to listen. My mistress frowns a little. In truth, she does not like the actual process of being examined, no more than she likes the various treatments he applies, but she tolerates them for the sake of his presence. I am sure he is aware of this, and he always responds to her complaints with as much gravity as he can muster. Together, they are like players in a comedy.

'Your chest is a trifle heavy,' he says finally. 'A dose of camphor should suffice.' It is his favourite remedy, and not one she is overly fond of. She barely manages to conceal her distaste.

'Very well, if I must,' she says with a sigh.

'It will clear your chest and raise your spirits,' he responds, snapping his case shut with authority.

'I should be grateful if it did not give me indigestion.' He appears not to notice this comment, and takes up his case in preparation to leave. 'Will you not stay on for lunch?' she asks, a note of irritation creeping into her voice.

'I apologise. I am needed in the village.'

'In the village?' says my mistress, raising her eyebrows. There are few in the village who can afford a physician's services. 'For whom?'

'The boy. The Long Boy. He has been overcome with fits.'

'How unfortunate,' she murmurs, her eyes once again flitting to the window. 'They say that she froze solid.' She turns to him. 'Is this true?'

Lucius blanches; the question clearly unsettles him. 'Such a thing is possible,' he says finally. 'By the time I saw her she was . . . thawed.'

My mistress shrugs, picks at her bedclothes. 'I suppose we should not pity her. She lived life as she chose.'

'No,' says Lucius quickly. He pauses, then deliberately relaxes his tone. 'She would not want our pity.' His voice trails off, followed by an awkward silence.

'She did not choose to die,' I say quietly. They both turn to look at me, and I feel the heat rise in my face.

I do not know what has prompted this thought, nor why I did not keep it to myself.

'No one does, my dear,' says my mistress pointedly. 'The Lord chooses for us.'

I do not reply, thinking only that Dora did not deserve such an end. Lucius looks at me and I am sure he reads my thoughts. He clears his throat.

'Any woman in her condition would have been at risk for such a fall,' he says quietly.

I raise my head to look at him. 'What do you mean?' I ask.

'She was with child,' he declares, after a pause.

'I did not know,' my mistress says, raising her eyebrows. She turns to me a little expectantly, but already my mind is distracted by the image of her lifeless body. Once again I see Lucius's hands travel loosely over her belly. Only a trained eye would have recognised her pregnancy; it was not discernible to me. But to my mother, who laid her out in death, it must have been apparent.

Chapter Three

It snows intermittently throughout the afternoon, and by the time I finish work the grounds outside the Great House have been frosted like a cake. My feet are among the first to mar the pristine whiteness covering the ground. As I hurry along the road towards Long Boy's cottage, the snow begins to fall anew, large wet flakes that cling to my eyelashes and clothes. I raise my face to the evening sky and the snow stings my skin with its icy, moist caress. As I reach the first few cottages on the outskirts of the village, I hear the shouts of children up ahead. The sky is dark but the snow itself lights their play. They have piled up a mound as tall as I am, and scramble over each other happily, oblivious of the cold. As I watch them tumble about in the dark, I cannot help but think of Long Boy in his bed, for he has never known the joy of child's play. He knew only his mother's love, and now even that has been taken from him.

By the time I arrive my shoes are wet through and my toes aching from the cold. It is my mother who answers my knock at the door. She is wearing a white apron, soiled from the day's work, and her forehead is smudged with ash from the fire. Her face is lined and heavy, but no more than usual, for it has been so all my life. Like me, she is small and neatly formed, though her waist has thickened with age. Her once-black hair has turned to grey, and she keeps it tightly bound in a linen cap.

The inside of the cottage is barely discernible in the semi-darkness, the only light coming from a few glowing embers in the fireplace. My mother presses a finger to her lips and motions me inside, where I can see Long Boy sleeping in his bed. A pan of water lies on a chair next to the bed, and a cloth is draped over his forehead.

'His fever is broken,' says my mother.

'The doctor was here?' I ask.

She gives a curt nod and picks up the bowl, carrying it to the front door and emptying it outside. When she returns she goes to the fireplace and stirs a pot hanging over the embers. The room smells of brewing herbs: I recognise the aroma of one of my mother's remedies.

'What did he say?'

She pauses before answering. 'He gave me camphor.'

'Did you use it?'

She purses her lips and nods to the boy. 'It was not needed.' My mother has little time for physicians and their cures, and has her own store of remedies made from ingredients she either grows or gathers. It is useless to argue with her over such things, so instead I move to the boy's side. His skin is pink in the firelight, almost luminescent, and his dark hair is damp with sweat, but he sleeps deeply and easily. I stand for a moment over him: his face is a curious mixture of youth and maturity. His cheeks are round and full, like that of a toddler, but already he sprouts a downy show of black hair upon his upper lip.

My mother busies herself at the table, moving quietly about with various preparations. After a moment I turn back to her.

'Why did you not tell me she was with child?'

She stops suddenly and looks at me, her face a mask. 'There was no need,' she says after a moment. 'The baby died with her. I am sure of it.'

I stare at her a moment. 'How long was she with child?' I ask.

'Some months. Five, perhaps six. She did not know.'

'But you did.'

My mother shrugs. 'Six,' she says.

'She kept it secret?' I ask a little incredulously. Dora had never before made a secret of her pregnancies. That she would do so now strikes me as strange.

'She did not want it known.'

'Why?' I demand.

My mother hesitates. 'She had her reasons,' she said finally. I stare at her expectantly. She looks at me and shakes her head. 'But I was not aware of them.'

I sigh and lower myself into a chair while my

mother continues with her work. She takes a bowl of bread dough from near the fireplace and turns it out on the table, punching it with vigour. I watch her turn and slap it for a minute, listen to the sound of each blow bounce off the stone mantel. When she is done she shapes it with her hands, patting and rotating it in her palms until it forms a wheel. I think of Long Boy and his appetite: who will make his bread tomorrow?

'Her death does not make sense,' I say.

'It was her time,' she says brusquely.

'You cannot believe that,' I reply. My mother purses her lips, but says nothing. I rise and look her in the eye. 'Why did she die?' I say. My mother stares at me a long moment.

'She met with fear,' she replies finally. 'It killed her.' She starts to turn away from me but I grab her arm.

'What do you mean?'

She glances over at Long Boy, then lowers her voice. 'Two weeks ago she came to see me. I have never seen her thus,' she says. 'She believed there was something wrong with the baby inside her. She claimed . . . it was the devil's child.' For the first time I see the fear in her eyes.

'What did she mean?'

My mother shakes her head. 'She would not say.'

I stare at her a moment. 'Have you spoken of this to anyone?'

'No.' She pauses. 'What good would come of it? She is dead.'

'Yes, but—'

She stops me with a shake of her head. 'You know as well as I what would happen were I to bring the devil's name into it,' she says, a little accusingly. Her eyes are flashing now, angry.

I look at her but the face I see is that of Goodwife Kemble, who was tried for witchcraft in our village not three years ago. She had fallen out with her former employer and was accused of casting spells over his household, resulting in the death of first his livestock, then his second son. Less than a fortnight after the altercation the boy succumbed to a mysterious fever that appeared suddenly and without warning. His cap was found buried in a dungheap behind her cottage, and this was the principal evidence used against her in court. At trial she admitted to base feelings against her former employer but swore that she had not consorted with the devil. She was an old woman, a spinster who had a reputation as a gossip and a scold, which served her poorly in the end. As a final test of her guilt, she was taken to the village pond where she was ducked repeatedly under the icy waters until she finally drowned.

My mother picks up a rush broom and begins to sweep the floor with vigorous strokes. She is right, it would be very risky for an older woman of the village to raise the devil's name in connection with any death. The magistrates are known to be swift in their condemnation and merciless in their sentencing of anyone connected to sorcery, and over the past decade I have heard tell of at least half a dozen women, most of them my mother's age or older, who have come to such an end.

'She must have told you *something*,' I insist, leaning forward.

My mother ignores me and continues sweeping. At that moment, her mean-spirited cat appears in the window and hisses at me. It must have followed her to Dora's cottage. Irritated, my mother waves the broom in its direction and the cat jumps past her, landing deftly beside the table where it pounces upon a scrap of suet. My mother opens the door and shoos the cat outside with her broom, before resuming her sweeping.

'Who fathered the child?' I ask.

My mother stops and looks at me. 'What kind of nonsense question is that?' she says dismissively. 'The entire village . . .' She throws her hand up in a sweeping motion.

'She must have known,' I say.

'How could she?' she says, then resumes sweeping.

I remain silent, watch her move about the room, then grab the broom and force her to look at me.

'What *exactly* did she say about the child?'

My mother purses her lips and searches the floor with her eyes. I have a sense that Dora's secrets are somehow trapped inside her, that once again it is my mother who must bring them forth into the world. Finally she raises her head and looks me squarely in the eye.

'She said that it would kill her.'

Chapter Four

I suppose that I have always been prone to melancholy. Even as a child they called me fanciful, for the world of my imaginings often seemed more real to me than any other, and it was certainly preferable. I was small and slight for my age, and as an only child was left to my own devices, for my mother's work often took her away for long periods of time. So from a very young age I was accustomed to solitary play, but I was not alone, for I surrounded myself with fairies, spirits and the like.

My mother regarded my fancies as ungodly, though they did not concern her overly until I reached the age of ten. By then I had developed certain fears as well; wind, high places and water were among them, so much so that for a time I would not wash, nor even drink, unless forced to do so. My mother feared my fluids were unbalanced, and for years she kept a close eye on all that came in and all that went out, giving me emetics, or tickling my throat with a feather, if she thought my humours were not soluble. Once she consulted a healer who was passing through on the road to London, and he told her to place a pan of urine beneath my bed at night, so that its odours should penetrate me while I slept. This we did for a time, until the stench became unbearable, or until she divined that the effect upon my humours was negligible. I never knew which but felt considerable relief when she finally abandoned the cure. In fact my health was generally better than her own, for in winter she often suffered colds, and twice when I was very young she experienced fits of the stone, which she passed after enduring many hours of agony in her bed.

For a time in my youth I had visions in my sleep, and my mother sought advice from both a cunning woman and a clergyman. The cunning woman lived in a neighbouring village and was known for miles around for her charms and prayers. She lived alone, her husband having died of smallpox, and people sought her out for all kinds of ailments, both physical and spiritual. I did not know her real name, but they called her Mother Hare, for she kept a rabbit's foot round her neck at all times, along with a sacred cross, to bring her luck and ward off evil. Mother Hare was old but not crooked as so many are, and though her face was lined, her eyes were clear and bright, and her smile winning. She lived in a tiny cottage on the outskirts of the village, and existed on the gifts of those who came to her for help. My mother and I travelled by foot to see her, leaving early in the morning and arriving at midday, and carried two loaves of bread, some boiled fowl and tallow candles as payment. I was anxious at the prospect of the visit, and walked slowly, my mother urging me on. But once inside her cottage I was instantly relieved, for she had an air of calm and quietude about her, the like of which I had not met before. I did not understand the prayers she spoke over me, for her words were intermixed with Latin, but I remember clearly the lay of her hand against my brow, smooth and cool like a cloth of fine white linen. Even my mother seemed affected by her presence, and when the prayers ended my mother clasped both her hands and appeared, for a moment, unable to speak. On the journey home I felt at peace, and that night I slept easily for the first time in many weeks. But after a fortnight of relative calm, the dreams returned.

This time she took me to a clergyman. Reverend Wickley presided over services at the Great House chapel, which served as church for our small parish. He hailed from the north and spoke with a strange accent, and had travelled the length and breadth of the kingdom before taking orders. It was said he'd been a pedlar in his previous life, and that he'd been married more than once, though these were only rumours. He married a yeoman's daughter soon after settling in our village, but his unfortunate wife died in childbirth within a twelvemonth. Shortly afterwards, he retained a young serving woman from a neighbouring village, who some said was more than generous in her provision, but as she rarely went out and had no family to speak of, the matter was soon forgotten. I saw her briefly in the yard the day we went to visit him, but when I asked my mother about her afterwards, she shrugged and said the girl was in God's service. Some years after, the girl in question disappeared and was never heard of again; it was rumoured she was with child and had run away to London.

I was twelve when my mother took me to see Reverend Wickley. I had often heard him preach and I always found his presence menacing. He was tall and dark and of an unusually good complexion, having evaded scarring by the pox, and was robust in his bearing, though his teeth were black and broken. It was clear that many of those in the congregation found his visage pleasing, and I was not very advanced in age before I perceived that women outnumbered men in attendance at holy service by several number. My mother, as always, was indifferent to such considerations, and was reverent without being devout.

It was nearly midsummer when we went to see him, and our days and nights had been overtaken by the heat. I had slept badly for a fortnight, waking often in a sweat and crying out while I slept, and my mother was growing increasingly uneasy. For my own part, the dreams did not trouble me overly; although I often woke during the night in an agitated state, by dawn I had usually fallen into the deepest of slumbers, so much so that my mother had to rouse me vigorously in the mornings. Rather than agitated I was somewhat enervated by day, but even this my mother took to be a sign that something was amiss, either in my body or my soul.

So it was we found ourselves on Reverend Wickley's threshold one blistering day. His look on seeing us was one of mild surprise: my mother was not overly religious, and I do not think she had ever undertaken a private consultation with him before, outside of her official capacity as midwife. And although she'd been determined to seek his advice, once again overcoming my objections, when we finally stood face to face with him, she appeared decidedly uncomfortable. Sensing her unease, the Reverend ushered us inside and led her to a chair.

'My good woman, pray be seated,' he said, taking her by the hand and leading her to a chair. 'Your colour is not well.'

Indeed her colour was not well, for it was the first time I could ever recall seeing her touch, or be touched, by a male personage, be he peasant or parson. And though he took her hand but momentarily, I perceived her recoil slightly, and it was clear to me (though not to him) that this had unsettled her more than the original purpose of our visit. I remained still until he turned to me and extended his hand, where upon I bolted for the only other chair in the room, thus avoiding unsettling her any further. After a moment she regained her colour and began to address him haltingly, telling him of my dreams, or visions as she called them, and of my inability to rouse at dawn, and of my general lethargy by day.

He listened to her most attentively and when she was finished he turned to me and subjected me to such intense scrutiny that I did blush beyond my control. He asked her my age, and questioned her as to my general health and humours as a child, and then, to my great embarrassment, asked her whether my menses had arrived, to which she replied with a curt, tight-lipped shake of the head.

He then turned to me and addressed me directly.

'These visions, of what do they consist?' he asked. They both looked at me, and at once the room felt suffused with heat; I felt at any moment my head might detach and float to the ceiling.

'Of demons and the like,' said my mother, after a moment's hesitation.

He turned to me again, his eyes narrowing slightly, and I perceived that his interest in me had suddenly heightened, as if I were no longer the same girl who had sat before him moments before.

'And these demons, what sort of appearance do they take?' he asked intently.

This time my mother was unable to reply, for I had never spoken to her in any detail of my dreams, and indeed did not always remember them myself in the morning. Often I recalled only fragments, hung like pictures in my mind. It was true enough that my sleep was haunted by demons. These were always in the shape of men, some I knew and some I didn't, whose natural appearance had been somehow altered in my dreams. Sometimes they were taller, sometimes shorter, sometimes with horns, sometimes with extra limbs and such. The Reverend Wickley himself had appeared on more than one occasion, once with teeth so large they hung below his lips. I hesitated a moment, unsure how to reply.

'They are a little like yourself, sir,' I said at last.

He exchanged a look of surprise with my mother. 'Are you saying that your demons appear with my likeness?' His voice had risen slightly and his eyes flashed with anger. My mother looked from me to him and back at me again, her eyes imploring.

'No, sir,' I stammered. 'It is only to say . . . that they are male. Like you. That is all.'

The Reverend instantly relaxed, the anger ebbing from his face, and leaned back. 'I see,' he said after a moment. I lowered my head and listened to my mother's laboured breathing. 'Do they . . . *harm* you in any way?' he asked slowly.

'They . . . hold my ankles,' I replied.

He raised an eyebrow quizzically. 'Your ankles? That is all?'

'Sometimes they pull on my head. From above,' I added. My mother looked at me with a puzzled expression.

'They pull at you from both ends?' he asked, a note of alarm creeping into his voice.

'No, sir. Just one end. Or the other.'

'And then?' he asked.

'And then I wake,' I said. 'And they are gone.'

'I see,' he said flatly, leaning back in his chair. In

truth I could not help but feel I'd somehow disappointed him. My mother seemed relieved, however, and gave a loud sigh, and then there was silence in the room. The sun broke through the clouds just then, and a beam of light came through the window, lighting up the wooden floor beneath my feet. My leather shoes glowed momentarily, then just as quickly the light vanished, and they looked dull and of no consequence.

'God has many tools available to him for our chastisement,' said the Reverend finally. 'Visions are just one of them,' he continued. 'Illness is another. You are very fortunate that in your case he has chosen the former and not the latter.'

'Yes, sir,' I mumbled, keeping my head well down.

'Praise the Lord,' murmured my mother.

'Praise Him indeed,' said the Reverend sternly. 'For He is worthy, and He has given you fair warning of His power.' He turned to my mother, who nodded her assent, then looked back at me. 'I recommend that you increase your attendance at holy service. And in addition, that you read and dwell upon the Holy Scriptures.'

I raised my head and looked quickly at my mother, who blinked several times and shifted uncomfortably in her seat. She hesitated, then spoke haltingly.

'If you please, Reverend, we have not the learning for such things.'

'My lady at the Great House would be delighted to assist,' he said. 'She reads Scripture daily to the maids and other folk under her service, and I have no doubt

that she would be happy to number you among them.'
He looked from me to my mother, who nodded.

'Yes, sir,' she said. 'And our thanks be with you.'

'The Lord forgives,' he said, turning his iron gaze
upon me, and for a split second I felt sure he knew of
my deceit, and that he had willed me into some
conspiracy of silence. Our eyes locked together and in
an instant he again altered to the visage from my
dreams, fangs and all. Then I felt my mother's hand
upon my arm, and as she pulled me out of the door, I
tore my gaze from his.

Once outside my senses returned. My mother chas-
tised me for my behaviour, but it was clear she was
relieved that the business was over and done with.
And she resolved from thenceforth that we should
attend Mass every evening, instead of thrice weekly as
we had previously, and that she would take me the
very next day to meet the lady he had spoken of, who
gave Scripture to the poor.

And that is how I first came to the Great House.

My dreams eventually subsided in their frequency,
though they did not cease altogether. But I kept them
to myself; the experience with Reverend Wickley
taught me to be more circumspect. I know now that
the world outside is an uneasy one, where fear and
suspicion are as likely to prevail as tolerance and
understanding.

The night I left my mother tending Long Boy, my
dreams returned. I dreamed that it was I who'd given

birth to the devil, not Dora, and that my mother had delivered me. The devil himself was not an infant, but a boy child of eight or nine years, with horns and teeth and eyes like blazing embers. He snarled like an animal, and fought and clawed his way out of my body. My mother gritted her teeth and grabbed him by the throat, and before I knew it she had stuffed him in a sack of hemp cloth and thrown it on the fire. The flames leaped and the bag burned with a vengeance. My mother smoothed her skirts and picked up a broom and began to sweep the floor, while I lay speechless with shock on the bed. When she was finished she took up the iron poker and jabbed at the still-glowing remains. Satisfied, she planted herself in a chair by the fire, the iron poker clutched tightly in her hand.

In all my life I had never experienced a dream of such vividness, nor one so complete in its conclusion of events. I woke in a cold sweat with a great, pitted feeling in my stomach, as if my insides had been torn from me in sleep. And I wondered what went through Dora's mind as she plunged towards the ice.

Was it fear she felt, or relief?

Chapter Five

I oversleep, and wake from the dream feeling heavy-headed. Outside my window, the morning sky is grey and threatening. Overnight the snow has turned to freezing rain. The trees are now so thickly iced that their heavy boughs droop and tremble in the wind. The cold reaches through my leaded window and envelops me like a sheath, causing me to shiver as I pull my woollen stockings on. I feel a stab of pain across my brow as I bend over, no doubt the residue from my nightmare. I must speak to Long Boy again as soon as possible. Perhaps he can shed some light on the tale my mother has related.

I finish dressing quickly and go directly to my mistress's chamber, for she likes me to attend her promptly in the mornings. When I arrive, she has dressed herself and is seated in front of her glass, attempting to arrange her hair, a task she normally leaves to me. I can see at once from her demeanour that her humours have improved and that she has resolved to be well. But to my horror she takes one look at my reflection in the glass and says my colour is poor, and bids me to sit down immediately. I am still uneasy from the night's events, it is true, and my eyes are swollen from oversleep, but aside from an agitated spirit I assure her I am fine. She does not listen to a word, as is her custom, but looks me over and pronounces me unfit for work, and insists on sending for Lucius against my protests.

She instructs me to lie down on a chaise longue in her antechamber, so as to spare both Lucius and me the embarrassment of receiving him in my bedchamber, then orders Cook to prepare an elderflower tonic at once. I tell her this will not be necessary (a sentiment Cook shares, evidently, from the expression on her face) but my mistress will not hear of my protests, and insists on tending me herself. She even undertakes a reading from the Scriptures to pass the time until Lucius arrives, though she struggles to see the page with her failing eyes.

Some time later Lucius bustles in with his usual fanfare, apparently unaware that he has been summoned on my behalf, rather than hers. He raises an eyebrow when she informs him, but gives a brief nod and turns to me. He examines me with care, out of deference to her, but in truth appears unimpressed, thus doubling my already acute embarrassment. My mistress hovers to one side as he takes my pulse.

'She is out of humour, is she not?' she demands of Lucius.

'Her colour is pale, it is true. And her pulse is a

trifle weak, but I can find no other evidence of ailment,' he replies in a clipped tone.

Lucius bids me open my mouth and examines my tongue and teeth, and peers down my throat as best he can, causing me not a little discomfort. My mistress strains to see over his shoulder, making me feel at once like a herd animal being sold at market. After a moment, Lucius straightens and replaces his instruments in their carrying case.

'One need only look at her to see that she is not herself,' says my mistress in a slightly defensive tone.

'Perhaps,' says Lucius inconclusively. He takes my hands and examines the palms, pressing on their centres with each of his thumbs. Then he takes my chin firmly in his hand and lifts it so as to look into my eyes.

'Her eyes are tinged with yellow,' says my mistress.

Lucius grunts in response but says nothing.

'It is a sure sign of green sickness,' she continues. 'She is of the age, to be certain.'

At this I blush so fiercely that I must lower my head. My mistress needs only to hear of some young woman being in a state of distress and she diagnoses a fit of green sickness, which occurs when a young maid's natural passions are left unattended.

'Please, mum, I am well,' I stammer. 'It is nothing but a touch of tiredness.'

Lucius clears his throat and stands. 'I suspect that she is right,' he says. 'But I will prescribe a remedy which will purge her of the green, should it indeed be present in her blood.'

My mistress gives a satisfied sniff and nods at me knowingly. I sigh and close my eyes for a moment. Lucius ferrets around in his black bag until he finds a vial with some greyish powder inside, and instructs my mistress in its preparation. He advises me to remain in bed for the remainder of the day, and says that he will look in on me the following morning on his rounds, a comment which quite evidently pleases my mistress, who would surely have him visit daily if she could. It occurs to me that she has invented the entire incident at my expense simply to create a diversion, but I am too tired to feel angry.

As Lucius turns to go she asks after the boy. He looks at her uncomprehendingly.

'The Long Boy,' she says.

He nods. 'I saw him first thing this morning. He is much restored. Eating now, and talking sense. The fever is gone. It appears my treatment was a great success,' he adds in a satisfied voice.

I think of the vial of camphor, sitting untouched on the table of the cottage, and of my mother's herbs. Lucius looks at me.

'Your mother has been very devoted in her attendance to him,' he adds in a measured tone.

'She was there this morning?' I ask.

He nods.

'You are very charitable, Lucius, to donate your services to such an unfortunate case,' says my mistress, perhaps a trifle goadingly.

Lucius turns slowly to her, his eyes narrowing

slightly, and appears to be weighing up his answer. 'She retained my services some time ago,' he says finally, one eyebrow raised.

'His mother?' asks my mistress.

Lucius nods.

'In the event that some misfortune should befall her, she did not want the boy left unattended.'

'She said this?' I ask, propping myself up on one elbow.

He turns to me. 'In so many words. It was extremely prudent of her, for she had no way of knowing,' he says matter-of-factly.

'No, of course not,' murmurs my mistress. 'How could she?' And with that she turns to me, and locks her gaze on mine. I feel the heat rise in my face, and my mistress looks at me strangely.

And then the room begins to spin.

When I regain consciousness, I am lying in my own bed, and the large, fleshy face of Cook is looming over me. Tufts of bushy grey hair fly from her cap, and a light dusting of flour has settled on one. Her dark eyebrows are knitted together with concern, and her meaty hands are heavy with the scent of lard. She wrings a rag out in a basin of cold water by the bed, and bathes my forehead with it, peering at me anxiously.

'What happened?' I ask.

She shakes her head and makes a sucking noise through the gap in her two front teeth. Cook is short on words but generous with sentiment; she never fails to make her meaning known. I notice that someone has loosened the cords of my underbodice and removed my kirtle. I start to sit up, but Cook gently pushes me back down onto the pillow.

'Not yet,' she says, turning away to rinse the cloth once again in the basin.

In a flash Lucius's words come back to me. Dora truly felt she was in danger of death, but why? What did she know about the child inside her? Was it possible that she had lain with the devil, as my mother had suggested? I did not believe such things were likely, though many in the village did. I believed in the powers of the cunning men and women: that certain people had an ability to influence their surroundings through particular means. I had seen evidence of this on more than one occasion. But of the devil's ability to assume a human form and father a child, this much I doubted, for even God himself did not achieve such things, and surely God must be more powerful than Satan. But if not the devil, then who? Dora had no enemies that I knew of. She lived in fear of no one.

Cook lays the cloth upon me once again, and I close my eyes. The images of last night's dream dance before me, particularly the face of the boy, his fearsome expression, and the sound of his howl as the sack hit the flames. I open my eyes to stop them and Cook looks down at me with concern.

'I must get up,' I say.

'And faint again? Not while I am here,' says Cook firmly.

'It is only a little tiredness. I slept poorly in the night, that is all,' I insist.

'Then you must rest now,' she says.

'Please,' I say imploringly. 'I do not wish to.' Cook looks at me suspiciously. She seems to sense that the prospect of sleep frightens me, for she sighs and offers an arm to help me rise. She helps me with my underbodice and kirtle, and pins my hair anew.

'Where is my mistress?' I ask.

'In her chamber,' says Cook.

'Please send word to her that I am much recovered,' I say. Cook raises an eyebrow at me quizzically. 'And that I should like to rest awhile longer in my room.'

Cook hesitates, then nods. I squeeze her hand in thanks, and slip out of the door.

When I arrive at Long Boy's cottage, I pause just outside. No doubt my mother still attends to him, and I prefer to speak to Long Boy without her present. I knock and enter, and she is indeed there, chopping herbs and onions, an iron pot simmering on a hook over the fire. Long Boy is asleep in bed, and in a glance I can see that Lucius is right, for his colour is much improved and his breath comes easily. My mother, however, appears overtired. Her movements are sluggish compared with her usual efficiency, and her face is tinged with grey.

'The boy is better,' she says, by way of greeting.

'I met Lucius this morning,' I tell her. She shrugs. 'You stayed the night?' I ask.

'I felt it best,' she says, indicating a wooden chair by the fire. I do not ask, but sense that she is unwilling to occupy Dora's bed.

'You must go home and rest,' I tell her.

'There is no need,' she says.

'He is over any danger now, you can see that.'

'She would want me to stay,' says my mother.

'*She* would be very grateful for all you've done. And would not wish you to put your own health at risk any more than is necessary,' I say firmly. 'I will stay with him until he wakes.'

My mother hesitates a moment. 'He must have broth,' she says.

'Yes of course.'

'And bread. And herbs. But no meat. He is not strong enough.'

'I understand.'

'I've made a tonic.' She indicates a jug on the table filled with murky brown liquid.

'As soon as he wakes,' I say, easing her into her coat.

'Above all he must rest,' she says. She stops and looks at me. 'What of the Great House?' she asks.

'I am not needed. My mistress is away,' I say.

She nods, relieved. From a very young age I have been able to deceive her with ease.

I take her arm and steer her out of the door. 'Go now and rest,' I say.

When she is gone, I finish chopping the salad herbs and add them to the pot by the fire. I check to see that the boy is deep in sleep, then begin a thorough search of the cottage. Aside from the bed and a trundle below it, the dining table and two chairs, there are two wooden trunks and a smaller chest. I cross the room and open the first trunk. Inside I find an extra set of bedlinen, washed and neatly folded, together with two man-size shirts, a pair of men's hose, two felt caps for Sunday wear, and a heavy woollen cloak which I have seen the boy wear on several occasions. The second trunk contains her own clothes: two gowns, one for every day, and one for field labour, her best gown having been used for the burial; two spare kirtles and caps, and a carved wooden rosary.

The boy stirs and I quickly replace the things. He does not wake, however, and I move on to the chest. It is a good deal smaller than the trunks, more a treasure box of sorts, with ornamental metal hinges, carved wooden handles and a floral pattern embossed in ivory upon the lid. When I try to open it, I am unable, as the lid appears to be fastened by some kind of hidden catch. I lift the box carefully and examine it from every angle, but can find nothing that resembles a release. Puzzled, I lay it down on the table and step back a few paces to view it from afar. This time something catches my eye: one handle is slightly larger than the other. I apply pressure to one side of the handle and it moves a hair's breadth, at the same time releasing the lid. I smile, pleased at the ingenuity and craftsmanship of the box, and wonder for a moment where she would have obtained such an object.

Inside I find a velvet pouch on top of a piece of folded linen cloth. I glance quickly at the boy and take out the pouch: the velvet is of deepest green, kept closed by a simple drawstring made of silk. I loosen the cord and remove an exquisite blue vial made of Venetian glass, about the size of my hand. My master has a collection of such glass in his library, and has travelled to London on several occasions to obtain more. I carefully loosen the cork, sniffing the contents. Though I am expecting perfume, I find to my surprise that it is oil of myrrh, a scent I know well, for my master makes frequent use of it as a tonic for his ailments. I replace the vial in the pouch, hesitate a moment, then tuck it inside my kirtle.

I take out the piece of fine linen cloth. When I unfold it, I see at once that it is an infant's nightdress, delicately embroidered with flowers along the sleeves and hem. The gown was no doubt ivory originally but has yellowed slightly with age. It must have been worn by Long Boy many years ago, and suggests a trace of sentimentalism in his mother which I would not have predicted.

Finally I remove a tiny silver picture frame which holds a miniature portrait of a woman I have never seen. She is young, not many years older than I am, and dark-haired, with a fine long nose and sharpish chin. She wears a deep crimson gown with an ivory-coloured overbodice and enormous sleeves that are exquisitely decorated. The gown is of a style popular some years before my birth; I recognise the type from portraits hanging in the Great House. In her hand the woman clutches a Bible and a rosary. I peer closely at the detail, for the rosary appears to be the same as the one I have just found in Dora's trunk, though it is difficult to know for sure, as the portrait is so small. I have heard talk of such miniature portraits, as they are presently very fashionable at Court, but this is the first one I have ever seen, and I marvel at the intricacy with which it has been painted. Indeed, my mistress has for some weeks been awaiting the arrival of a young painter from Flanders who specialises in such commissions, as she desires one for her collection.

On the reverse of the frame is etched a tiny signature which I cannot make out, for the silver has tarnished badly with age. I turn it over and stare again at the woman in the tiny frame, and this time it strikes me that she shares a few similar features with Dora: mainly in the shape of the mouth, which is wide and full, and in the eyes, which are large and penetrating in their gaze. I glance over at the boy; the woman in the portrait must be his grandmother. He, too, shares a trace of resemblance to the portrait about the mouth and eyes, though that is all.

The boy coughs in his sleep and I quickly close the lid of the box and replace it. I move to his side as he stirs and wakes, blinking several times. He looks at me and yawns.

'Are you hungry?' I ask.

'Where is the other woman?' he says. He has

53

known my mother all his life and yet he does not refer to her by name.

'My mother has gone home to rest,' I tell him. 'She will return later.'

His eyes drift to the bread on the table. I rise and fetch him some broth from the pot simmering over the fire. He is still weak and I must help him sit up, but I am relieved when he is able to feed himself. He eats the soup hungrily, noisily, and asks me for some bread. I break off a hunk and give it to him. I wait while he finishes and then take the bowl. He lies back against the pillow, his eyes darting restlessly about the room.

'What happened?' he says.

'You had a fever,' I tell him. 'But it is gone now.'

'Who else was here?' he says.

'The doctor,' I reply. 'He came yesterday, and again this morning.'

'I have seen him here before,' he says. He picks at a feather poking out from the bedclothes.

'Your mother asked him to look after you,' I tell him.

'My mother?' He looks up at me expectantly.

'Before she died,' I add. Can it be that he does not remember? He looks past me at the wall for several moments. I draw a chair up to his bedside and sit down. I hesitate a moment, unsure how to proceed.

'Long Boy, your mother carried a child when she died,' I say slowly. 'Did you know of this?' He looks at me uncomprehendingly. 'In her belly,' I explain. 'She had an unborn baby in her belly.' Inadvertently my hands go to my own belly, and Long Boy follows them with his eyes. We both stare at my hands for a moment, splayed across my belly, until I feel self-conscious and remove them.

'What happened to it?' he asks.

'It died when she did,' I tell him gently.

'Why?' he says.

'Because an unborn baby cannot live without its mother,' I explain.

'Did you see it?' he asks intently.

I shake my head slowly. 'No.'

He frowns. 'Then how can you be sure?'

I hesitate, and I realise that I cannot be sure of anything. 'The doctor told me,' I say finally.

He appears satisfied with this answer, and looks down at the covers once again.

'The baby had a father, Long Boy,' I continue. He flashes me a questioning look. 'All children do,' I say, by way of explanation.

'I don't,' he says immediately.

I bite my lip. 'No. But this baby did.'

Long Boy ponders this a moment. 'Where is he?'

'I do not know,' I say.

He nods and makes an odd grinding noise with his teeth, as if he is preoccupied.

'This baby's father,' I tell him. 'I should like to know who he is.'

'Why?' he says.

I take a deep breath, let it out slowly. Why indeed? I

can think of no answer suitable for someone of his age.
'Because,' I say finally.

He nods, but does not realise I am asking him for
the answer. I lean forward, catch his gaze.

'Did any one man come to visit more than the
others?' I ask.

Long Boy's eyes come to rest on the vial of camphor, still lying on the table. 'He came,' he says.

I nod. 'More than the others?'

'No,' he replies.

I frown. My instinct tells me that Lucius is not the
man I seek. Then I remember the glass vial hidden
under my kirtle. Slowly I withdraw it and take the vial
from its pouch, holding it up for him to see. He
clearly recognises it, for his eyes flicker briefly to the
wooden box near the fireplace, then back at me. I
blush a little.

'This was your mother's?' I ask.

He shakes his head slowly. 'It was his.'

'The doctor's?' I ask, confused.

'No. The crooked one.'

He speaks of my master, with his crooked spine.
'He came here often?' I ask.

The boy nods.

'More than the others?'

He shrugs. 'It is possible.'

'Did she . . . favour him?'

He frowns then. 'Why would she?' he says in an
accusing tone.

'I do not know,' I say to placate him. 'I only wish to

know a little more.' His face relaxes a little.

'Was she . . . afraid of him?' I ask cautiously.

He gives me another dark look, as if this suggestion is even more offensive. 'No,' he says. 'She feared no one,' he adds, more than a hint of pride creeping into his voice.

I nod, smile a little at his loyalty.

'She was strong,' he continues. 'Stronger than all of them.'

'Of course she was,' I say, and know it to be true. We sit in silence for a moment, and my mind reaches back to a time as a child when I came upon her in the forest. She was bathing in the river a short distance from the village when I spotted her through the undergrowth. At once I was entranced by the sight of her naked flesh. Her back was turned to me and I saw that her shoulders were broad and muscled and as smooth as ivory. I watched as she scooped water over her head with a small wooden bowl, tilting her head right back, her hair stretching nearly to her waist in a glistening ribbon of wetness. She closed her eyes to the flow but kept her mouth open wide, allowing the river to course right through her. Over and over she doused herself and I stood rooted to the spot, unable to tear my eyes from the sight of her, even more unwilling to reveal my presence lest she stop. I did not breathe or stir until she had dried herself and gone, and only then did I emerge from the thicket, like a fawn at dusk, to kneel beside the river's edge and dip my fingers into the icy waters that had caressed her only moments before.

Long Boy has lost interest in our little talk, and I am left with only the spit and crackle of the fire. He keeps his silence in the corner, curling like a leaf towards the wall, while I ponder his answers. Although I had not been aware that my master frequented this place, the news does not surprise me, for he is a man like any other, even if his spine is bent. Despite his mother's wishes, he has never sought a wife, though there was talk in the village many years ago of a match. With youth and wealth, he might have found a woman who would tolerate his deformity, but having lost the former this now seems exceedingly unlikely. And, too, there is the matter of his character, which can only be described as eccentric, though perhaps this is unfair, for his deformity has resulted in his isolation from society.

At any rate, who would choose him as the father of her children? To marry such a man would entail considerable risks on the woman's part. She would live in perpetual fear of monstrous births, for it is known that those who are disfigured are many times more likely to produce deformities among their off-spring. Perhaps this is what Dora feared: a monstrous foetus inside her, and the risk that it might kill her in childbirth.

I dwell upon this notion for a time. If she had good cause to believe the child was his and was malformed, she would be right to fear a dangerous labour. Pregnancy is a calamitous journey at the best of times, and many women perish from the birth of normal, healthy babies, let alone monstrous ones. Even my mother lives in fear of such cases, for on the rare occasions when she has delivered a malformed child, the labour has been both prolonged and exceedingly tortuous for the mother. She is forever advising those under her care to take precautions against such births, believing fervently that they can be prevented by a woman's conduct. According to my mother, if a woman harbours perverse thoughts when she lies with a man, or indeed dwells too long upon strange objects, this can alter the development of the child within. Or if she lies with a man during her monthly courses, this too can result in death or deformity of an unborn child. Those who craved unnatural substances such as earth or coal in their diet also run such risks. There are many tales of such women being delivered of worms, toads, mice, even serpents. Indeed, the perils of childbirth are so numerous and so varied, I have often felt that it is a wonder any woman is prepared to undergo them.

But this was not the case with Dora, who throughout my childhood was pregnant more often than she was not. Indeed I cannot remember her as anything but great-bellied, though in truth her figure altered little, regardless of her condition. She was truly built for childbearing, with magnificent wide hips that rolled with grace when she walked, and a frame that was broad and square. Her belly, though indeed great, was never out of proportion to the rest of her, and her neck was long and surprisingly delicate given the size of her frame. Her eyes were large and luminous and, like a spring sky, changed colour with the sun. Even in death her appearance had been striking, as if God had claimed her just as she was.

Despite this, her births were dogged by misfortune. Most of her children died during labour, though one or two survived a short time before illness claimed them. With the exception of Long Boy, who was born when I was nine, I cannot recall any living beyond a few days. She buried them all behind her cottage, and asked God for his blessing, even if as bastard children they were not entitled to a proper Christian burial. She had not conceived a child in recent years, however, and I, like many others, believed that she was past the time of childbearing.

But Long Boy is right: fear was not in her nature. She regarded her pregnancies as both right and natural, and believed that God would not spurn either her or her children in the end. It seems clear to me from his response that Long Boy did not know of her condition, nor of her reasons for alarm. And while I am disappointed I am not surprised, for like any good mother she took steps to shelter him from the outside world and its dangers. If I am to unravel the questions surrounding her death, I shall have to seek my answers elsewhere, for I sense that there is little more to be learned from him directly.

My mother returns at dusk, appearing in some degree refreshed. The boy seems relieved when she enters, and she goes to him directly, spanning his forehead with her hand to check for fever.

'He is fine,' I say. 'I gave him the tonic.' They both ignore me, she concentrating on the feel of his brow. After a moment she releases him and nods.

'I am grateful for your help,' she says a little tersely. 'You can return now to the Great House.'

I hesitate a moment, watch her move to the fire, give the pot a stir. She cannot stay here indefinitely, but she is not likely to leave him thus. What will she do when he is recovered? I wonder. She lights a candle and places it on the table, then seats herself by the fire and takes out a ball of new-spun wool and her knitting needles. My mother's hands are never idle, and they fly about the needles like two swallows worrying a nest. The boy lies peacefully in the corner, and I hear him sigh as I put on my coat and slip out of the door, leaving the two of them to their silence.

In the scullery of the Great House, Cook is scolding Little George, the roasting boy, for allowing a joint to burn. When I enter, she leaves him cowering and comes towards me, wiping her hands on her blood-stained apron.

'You were overlong away,' she says.

'My mistress?' I ask.

'I had to keep her from your room,' she scolds me. 'I told her you were deep in sleep.'

'I am grateful,' I reply.

'Aye,' she says with a grimace, waving me away. I dash up the rear stairs and hasten to my room. Once inside I remove my kirtle and lay it on the bed, then I take the glass vial out of its pouch to examine it once more. Just as I do, I hear a soft knock on the door. Quickly I lie down on the bed, shoving the vial out of sight beneath my kirtle. My mistress enters and I feel my face flush, though I manage to smile at her in greeting.

'You're awake,' she says.

'Yes. I am much improved.'

'I am glad to hear of it,' she says with a nod. Her eyes flicker briefly around the room searching for a place to sit, and for a moment I fear that she will sit upon the kirtle, but to my relief she settles herself on the wooden chest at the foot of the bed.

'Lucius gave you a fright, I think,' she says a little archly.

'I was . . . overcome for a moment. I cannot think why,' I say. 'It was silly of me,' I add with a smile.

'Was it?' She raises an eyebrow. 'At times our minds and bodies are in complete accordance. If one succumbs, so does the other.'

'I suppose so,' I say, shifting awkwardly.

'Still,' she continues, 'if you consider it, her death is not so very surprising. The great-bellied woman lived in a state of perpetual sin, my dear. She must have known that God would claim her in the end,' she says pointedly.

'Yes, of course,' I murmur.

'We shall dwell no more upon it,' says my mistress, reaching over to pat my hand. She rises, and as she does she accidentally dislodges my kirtle, which lies folded at the foot of my bed. It slides to the floor and the vial hits the wooden boards with a thump.

'How clumsy of me,' she says, bending down to retrieve the kirtle, and as she picks it up she notices the vial. She holds it up to me.

'This is Edward's. Wherever did you find it?'

'On the path outside the house, mum,' I stammer.

She holds it up to the candlelight, admiring it for a moment. 'He lost it some years ago. I was terribly disappointed, as I'd purchased it myself from a dealer in London.'

'It is very beautiful,' I say.

'Perhaps one of the servants took it,' she says with a sigh, disregarding in her way the fact that *I* am a servant. 'I shall take it to him immediately,' she says, pleased at the prospect. 'And you must rest,' she says firmly. 'I only wished to ascertain that you were out of danger.' She pauses then and turns to face me one last time. 'Remember we must be vigilant with both our physick *and* our soul,' she says pointedly. 'The one cannot survive without the other.'

'Yes, mum.'

She leaves me then, with a little nod of condescension, and I am left holding her words.

Chapter Six

The following day I return to my duties. I am anxious to confront my master about the vial at the first opportunity, though it is not clear to me how I should do so. My mistress has received word of the impending arrival of the portrait painter and is busy making arrangements for his accommodation. She consults me over the suitability of his rooms, not wishing him to stay among the servants, as he has sat with royalty and her second cousin is his patron. But neither does she wish for him to be accommodated in the guest wing, for it is truly sumptuous, and by rights his status as a painter, even a talented one, places him only slightly higher than that of a craftsman. I suggest that he be given the tower room, above the library, for it is both apart from the servants' quarters and austere in its decoration. It also benefits from much sunlight, and I remind her that such matters are important to a painter. She nods at this, and instructs the houseman to move a bed into the room at once.

I also propose that the painter might appreciate

some volumes of history in his quarters, as he is due to remain for some days while he carries out his commission. My mistress agrees, and so I hurry to the library, where I know my master will be passing time among his books.

I am short of breath by the time I reach the tower, not so much from tiredness as from anticipation, and I pause just outside the library door, my heart thumping in my chest. I can hear my master moving about inside; he has a peculiar shuffling gait due to one leg being slightly shorter than the other. I knock and enter when he bids me to, and he turns to face me, his hair dishevelled and his eyes a little wild. Unlike his mother, he does not take much notice of his attire, and dresses in a melancholy manner, almost entirely in black, sometimes wearing the same dark tunic for several days at a time. He has a small moustache, which he is fond of stroking with his thumb and forefinger, and wears a tall, floppy, broad-brimmed hat whenever he goes out, lending him the appearance of a minstrel. His eyes are his most attractive feature, being large and round and tawny-coloured, with long curly lashes like a woman's. But what one notices most about him is his shape, for he is small in size, and his left shoulder protrudes sharply upward past his ear, so that his neck and head are almost always at a slight angle, a fact which I have always found unsettling when he speaks to me. That and his manner, which can only be described as somewhat absent, as if he is in a state of perpetual distraction.

He looks at me now in that slightly vacant way, as if his eyes are upon me but his vision has gone elsewhere, and I explain that I have come to borrow books on behalf of my mistress.

'What sort of books?' he asks sceptically, as my mistress keeps her own collection of psalms and Scripture in her antechamber, and is not fond of any other.

'History, sir. Or geography perhaps. They are for the portrait painter,' I add. 'For his amusement.'

'Ah,' he says, and shuffles slowly to the far side of the room, selecting half a dozen volumes from a shelf. 'These might interest him, if he is the reading sort, though he may well be illiterate. Many of them are, you know.'

'Yes, sir,' I reply, taking the books from him. He moves over to his desk then, and at the same time our eyes both light upon the vial, resting on the silken pouch on top of his desk. In an instant his face has dropped its vacant look.

'I owe you many thanks,' he says. His gaze drops down to the vial. 'It is indeed very precious to me, and I am grateful for its safe return.' He looks at me a little expectantly then, and I can only imagine a half-smile. 'My mother said you found it on the path . . . I cannot imagine how it came to be there.'

I take a deep breath before replying. 'No, sir, I did not. It was given to me by Dora before she died. She desired that it be returned to you . . . in the event that any misfortune should befall her.'

My master lowers his eyes, stares at the vial, loses himself inside it for a moment. 'I see. Then I must thank you doubly for your discretion,' he says, his voice barely above a whisper.

'She had some knowledge that death was near,' I say, moving towards him slowly. 'Indeed she feared that it was imminent.'

He frowns, his eyes cloudy with confusion. 'But her death was an accident.'

'One that she prepared for,' I reply. We both stare at each other for a long moment.

'What are you saying?' he asks.

I shrug. 'I only wish to know the truth.'

He pauses, his fingertips resting lightly on the desk, and just then his body sways almost imperceptibly. 'The truth is that I feel her loss acutely,' he says finally, sinking down into his chair and burying his hands in his hair. He stays this way for several moments, the room so quiet I can hear the ticking of the timepiece in the corner. 'But I know nothing of her death,' he says finally.

I wait a moment, ponder my options.

'Perhaps you knew she was with child,' I offer.

His face freezes. 'No,' he says, his voice crackling like fine paper. 'No, I did not.'

And I believe him, for there is a time when lying is not possible, when the flesh and fluids within us betray all our truths. This is when I ask my final question, the one I have been waiting to ask.

'The baby she carried, could it be . . .' I hesitate,

summon my courage. 'Is it possible that it was yours?'

He looks at me and his eyes slowly bloom with pain. His face twitches and his chest heaves. Then he shakes his head, just barely, from side to side. 'Such a thing could not be possible,' he says, his voice barely audible.

My mouth is dry like cotton. 'Forgive me, sir,' I whisper.

Then I take his books and run from the room.

By the time I reach the main house I am drenched with fear. I have never seen my master thus, and though I do not fear for the sake of my own person, I am nonetheless frightened for his. Our bodies are the safe house of our passions, but there are limits to what they will contain. If the house becomes too full, it will unburden itself in some manner: either by sickness, or by deed. In truth, the severity of his response confounds me. Though my question clearly caught him unawares, it was not ill-founded, for he is a man like any other. And though I took some liberties in the asking, I did so with the knowledge that theirs was no casual liaison, for he himself had just revealed to me the depth of his affections. Indeed, Dora touched so many in our midst, that it now begins to seem as if she spun a dense web of loyalty around her, one so vast that I cannot step in any direction for fear of tripping up against the thread of her presence.

And I myself am caught within the web, for like my master I feel her loss acutely. Why else do I seek an answer to the riddle of her death?

At the end of the day, when I return to my room, I find a plain-wrapped parcel waiting on my bed. When I open it a small cloth purse drops into my lap, together with a note on white parchment. Though he does not sign it, I recognise my master's hand. The message reads simply: 'Please deliver this safely to her son.' I open the purse and empty its contents onto my bed. It is more money than I have ever seen – indeed it is more than I have ever *dreamed* of seeing. What does he hope to buy with this money? I wonder. Is it the price of my silence, or the cost of his guilt? I count it slowly, carefully, partly to be sure of its value, but partly just to have the feel of it in my hands. Then I return it to the purse, which I stow beneath my bedclothes. Tomorrow I will take it to the boy. But tonight I will sleep upon it, and dream the dreams of misers.

Chapter Seven

W hen I was a child, I went often to the great-
bellied woman's house, to sit upon the hearth
and listen to her stories. She was an accomplished
teller of tales who could spin whole worlds with only
a few long strands of words. The stories she told were
strange and exotic, unlike any I have heard before or
since: tales of people and places far across the sea, and
of animals unknown within our shores. These stories
lingered with me, and many are buried still within my
mind. They come to me now in fragments, often when
I least expect them, like uninvited guests. But they are
not unwelcome, as they bring with them part of her: a
sense of mystery and of possibility, coupled with that
peculiar blend of strength and calmness which was her
hallmark. For she was all these things to me, and I
suppose to many others as well.

I remember a tale of a great plumed bird who lived
high upon a mountain above the treetops, whose feet
never once came to rest upon the soil. The bird was
proud and kept to itself, only occasionally allowing the

people who lived in the village far below to catch a glimpse of its rare and beautiful plumage. One day a great hunter came to the mountain, and hearing of the marvellous bird, determined to capture it for its beautiful feathers. He told the unwitting people of the village that he would like to see the bird, but when he asked them to describe it, each gave a different account of its beauty. Some said its feathers were green and luminescent, like those of a peacock, while others said it was bright red with streaks of yellow and orange, like the setting sun. Still others said its body was black as coal, with snow-white tail feathers that flashed among the leaves when it flew. The hunter was confused and, deciding that the people were deliberately misleading him, resolved to find the bird himself. He climbed the mountain and for three days and nights remained hidden in the underbrush. On the fourth day he gave up hope and began his descent, when suddenly he caught a glimpse of a winged creature of such extraordinary beauty it made him gasp. He nearly forgot his purpose as he watched the bird soar and dive among the trees, but finally came to his senses and took aim with his bow and arrow. He heard a cry and saw the bird plummet towards the ground, but when he reached the spot where it should have landed, he found only a crow, pierced through the heart by his arrow, dead as a stone.

He picked up the crow and descended the mountain with great sadness, knowing as he did that the bird of his dreams was lost to him forever. When he reached the bottom, he hid the dead crow in his pack, and gathered the people of the village around him. He told them they were indeed blessed to have such a thing of beauty in their midst, and instructed them to revere it always. The people nodded and were relieved, secure in the knowledge that the bird would remain with them forever. The hunter left that land and never returned, and the people of the village kept their pride in the wondrous creature that lived among them.

Dora spun her stories with such intensity that she often left me breathless. Her pale eyes flashed with the excitement of the telling, and her long fingers rose and fell before her in an animated fashion. At these times she seemed to carry the heartbeat of armies within her ample breast – she seemed more alive to me than anyone or anything I had ever encountered in my own barren corner of the world. But what struck me most was how she differed from my mother, who though capable was unfailingly taciturn and circumspect, and did not trust the world beyond her threshold. My mother had no vision of life outside our little village; she did not dream of faraway lands or foreign peoples, nor did she aspire to any life other than her own. She accepted Dora for what she was, but granted her no other past. Once when I asked her why Dora had come across the sea, she looked at me a little strangely, as if I had spoken some heresy, and said that Dora had found her place within our village. 'But what of her own people?' I persevered. 'We are her people,' replied my mother, and with that she rose and turned her back on me, as if to stifle any further questions in my mind.

So I took my questions to Dora herself, asking her why she'd come so far across the water to settle in a strange land. She looked straight at me then, and her expression deepened, as if I'd vanished right before her eyes – for suddenly her face was taut with memory. She stayed that way for several moments, and then she blinked and looked at me anew. 'The world holds many lives for us,' she said finally. 'And in the end, I chose to lead this one.' She spoke slowly, choosing her words with care, as if the truth was too fragile to reveal. Or as if she must temper her words for my ears.

As a child of nine or ten, the idea that one could choose one's destiny made me almost dizzy with desire. I was too ignorant, too naive, or perhaps too stubborn to see how uncomfortably this notion sat within my mother's understanding of God or man or the nature of things. I knew only that it was strange and desirable. Now the idea frightens me, for I have learned with age that it contains seeds of truth and possibility. And there are times when I feel the stirrings of my childhood swell and rise within me, but always they are accompanied by fear, so much so that I often think that there are two people who dwell within me: my mother and myself.

I wake in the pre-dawn light feeling stiff and uneasy. Half asleep, I grope beneath my pillow for the purse

of gold, but my fingers scrape the sheet and claw at
nothing. I sit bolt upright, rubbing my eyes, wondering if I dreamed of its existence. And then I check the
floor beside my bed, where I see that it has fallen
during the thrashings of my sleep. I reach out to
retrieve it, and clutch it to my breast, my heart
beating wildly. For the first time it occurs to me that
to have so much wealth in one's possession is perhaps
a mixed blessing. What will it mean for the boy?

I rise and dress, stowing the purse deep within my
petticoats. I have no other alternative for its safe-
keeping, as I will not have an opportunity to take it
to the boy until that evening, and I do not wish to
leave it in my room. Then I smooth my skirts and go
below to take my breakfast with the others, the
money brushing up against me like a whisper. When
I reach the great hall the others are already hovered
over breakfast. A bitter draught buffets their faces
this morning, curtailing the normal talk and laughter
at the table. The two girls are seated together in
their usual place at one end, heads bowed and
shoulders just touching. They remind me of two
rodents worrying a biscuit. Alice, the elder of the
two, is one year my junior but behaves as if she is
half my age. The eldest daughter of a yeoman farmer
in the village, she is short and heavy-set with a
ruddy round face and eyes set deep within their lids.
She wears her straw-coloured hair in a long thick
plait down her back, and likes to toss her head about
for emphasis, causing the plait to jump and writhe

under her cap, like an angry snake. Lydia, the laundry maid, is two years younger, though much the more sensible of the two. She is not unpretty, though her face already bears the burden of hard labour, and her hands are rough and reddened from overuse of lye.

Little George, the turnspit, sits next to her, his eyes still filled with sleep. He wears a long knitted scarf wrapped round and round his neck which reaches nearly halfway up his face. He is an orphan whom my mistress rescued from the poorhouse, though he appears not to notice and persists in his misery. The youngest of the lot, he is not yet twelve, the same as Long Boy, though the two could not be more different. For a moment, I see Long Boy seated in his place, but the image quickly fades, for I cannot imagine Long Boy taking orders, much less carrying them out. He is far too much her son. I take a seat next to Little George, who shifts uncomfortably, then resumes eating.

The manservants, four in all, group themselves round the other end of the table. Nate and Joe are barely more than shaving age, stable hands who have been here less than six weeks and may not last the winter, judging by the restless look in their eyes. From time to time they leer at the girls, who pull faces in return, and then dissolve into giggles. My master's manservant Josias is much older and has lived all his life in the Great House. Indeed he was born within its walls and would no doubt perish were he forced to live outside them. He is quiet-spoken and loyal, like his father before him, but is not without some influence, as befits his position. Finally, there is Cook's nephew Rafe, a sort of Jack-about-the-house, who is smarter than the rest, and not to be trusted. He and I have crossed swords on more than one occasion, normally when I have caught him out for some wrongdoing. But he is under Cook's protection, though some day he will no doubt push her to the limit, as she frequently reminds him.

In all we are a motley crew, and I cannot help but wonder as I take my breakfast what would happen were I to spill the contents of the purse upon the centre of the table. Josias would pay no heed, as he is more than happy with his station, but for the others it would constitute an open door. And yet, what would they make of it, or more importantly, it of them? It would not alter their person: Alice would remain rough-skinned and heavy-set with her nose a little upturned; Nate would still carry the scars of pox, and Joe his crooked teeth. And what of Little George, would it relieve his misery? I doubt it, for all the gold coins in the world could not raise his parents from the grave. Perhaps Rafe would make something of it, for he has more imagination than the rest. But he is also impetuous, and it might well lead him down a path of wickedness and sin.

And so I keep the money stashed beneath my skirts, for it is safe there, and can do no harm.

My mistress rings her bell and I quickly finish my breakfast and rise. Cook has prepared a tray for her, and now I take it up with me. When I reach her chamber she is seated in front of her dressing table with a frown. She wears only her nightclothes, with a loose velvet dressing gown for warmth, and her hair is uncombed. When she sees me enter she makes a face of mock horror at her own reflection, then sighs and turns to me with a rueful smile.

'They say he is accomplished in the art of camouflage,' she says. 'He will have to be, in my case.'

It takes me a moment to realise to whom she is referring. The painter arrived late the previous evening, and is due to start work almost immediately. He will paint two miniatures of her, and a larger portrait for the great hall, and another of my master, if he will allow it. My mistress has not had her portrait done since her marriage, more than thirty years ago. It is customary for ladies to have their portraits painted with their children when they are still young, but it is said my master's father would not allow it, owing to his son's disfigurement.

I place the tray on the small round table by the window. Indeed we will have a task transforming her, but what make-up and fine garments cannot conceal, no doubt a paintbrush can. I stand behind her at the mirror and place my hands on her shoulders, concentrating on the look I should like to achieve before morning is out. She bites her lip and eyes me nervously: she is entirely in my hands, a feeling I must admit to liking. I smile a little to reassure her. 'We had better get to work,' I say. 'We have much to do.'

I begin with her make-up. The gown she has chosen is heavily embroidered, and no doubt it will overtire her if she is forced to wear it long. And the lace ruff she has chosen is so absurdly tall as to be almost unwearable. She has seen a similar one upon a portrait of the Queen, and had it copied by her tailor especially for this occasion. I begin to coat her cheeks with ceruse, mixing it with white of egg and applying it in layers until it entirely conceals the true colour of her skin. The process takes some time, as each layer must dry before the next is applied, and she passes the time in between by nibbling gingerly at a roll. When the base has been laid, I use henna and a fine brush to do her eyes, giving her eyebrows a slightly higher arch than usual, which pleases her enormously. I also paint a discreet mole on one cheek, the fashion at Court these days, and with a blue crayon I trace a vein snaking down her neck towards her bosom, which will be partially but modestly exposed by the squared neck of her bodice. Finally I rouge her cheeks ever so slightly with cochineal, as she is not overly fond of colour, and paint her lips a bright crimson. The entire process takes me nearly an hour, and when I am finished she is still uneasy, as her hair and garments remain undone, and the success of one without the other is limited at best.

'Trust me,' I say, patting her hand in reassurance. She gives a small embarrassed wave of her hand in response.

'I feel like a bride,' she says a little sheepishly.

'And you shall look like one before I'm through,' I respond.

We both know that I am lying.

The hair and headdress come next. First her own hair must be oiled so that it will lie flat upon her skull, then the wig must be applied and dressed. She has several and today has chosen her favourite, a very pale shade of auburn which, it must be said, becomes her. Once the wig is on she begins to relax a little, as it is now possible to foresee the final outcome. I tease and comb the curls into place, then carefully pin the headdress, a delicate tiara festooned with jewels which she has borrowed for the occasion, as her own failed to please her. She can barely move her head once it is on, as it sits rather precariously atop her curls, but her movements will be further hampered by the lace ruff.

We pause to rest then. It is past mid-morning and the sun is shining, which will no doubt please the painter, who is scheduled to arrive in her chamber at noon. She rings for some refreshment, which Alice brings on a tray, and the girl is nearly struck dumb by the sight of her mistress in jewelled headdress. I pour out ale for us both and when she takes a sip of hers she leaves faint marks of red upon the cup.

Her gown and underskirts have been newly pressed, and we begin the laborious process of removing her nightclothes and putting them on, taking extra care not to disturb her make-up or hair. First I carefully slip her best chemise over her head. It is finely spun of bleached white linen and will protect her elaborate outerwear from bodily secretions. Then comes a flannel petticoat for warmth, as she is bone-thin with age and suffers acutely from cold in winter. Her corset is extra fine, made of satin and linen with whalebone stays and a long central pocket into which I insert an ivory busk. Her body stiffens as I do so, and she draws in a breath at the effort of remaining erect. The corset is cut long, as is the current fashion, and has little loops at the bottom which will hold her farthingale in place. She prefers a French farthingale to the Spanish type; it, too, is made with whalebones, the skirt falling in a dramatic A from her hips. Finally I attach the bolster just above her hips. Hers is larger and more pronounced than my own, and dwarfs her measurements, but the effect pleases her. My mother has no time for such accoutrements, and is forever lecturing those in confinement to abandon them.

Next my mistress dons her partlet and kirtle, the latter with an elaborately embroidered front section to match the bodice of her gown. The gown itself is made of ivory-coloured silk and is ornately beaded and decorated in a floral pattern. She has worn it only twice before: once to a ball on a nearby estate and once when she travelled to view a royal progress. The sleeves are full and trimmed with exquisite French lace at the cuffs, so delicate it reminds me of spun sugar. She has chosen an uncharacteristically simple ivory brooch with matching earrings, a wedding present from her husband. I suspect its selection is due more to piety than fond remembrance. Finally I attach the ruff, an elaborate cloudy concoction which rises from the point of each shoulder and arcs across her back, towering well above her ears. Once it is in place we both draw a breath in admiration. The effect is indeed regal, and I can see from her demeanour that it pleases her. I glance at the timepiece on her mantel; there are still thirty minutes before the painter is due to arrive. She raises one hand as if to rise and I grasp it firmly in order to assist her. She stands and once again admires her reflection, then suggests that we take a turn about the house. It is a somewhat ludicrous notion, as there is no one but servants about, and this the likes of Little George and foolish Alice. But she is not to be deterred, and so I take her arm to steady her, and we begin our little progress.

We go first to the kitchen, so she can instruct Cook about the midday meal. This is entirely unnecessary, as Cook has complete run of the kitchen and takes orders from no one, and anyway my mistress has no interest in culinary matters, but we both know it is the hub of the house. When we enter, Little George is duly turning meat and Cook is patting out some pastry for a pie. Both freeze at the sight of her, Little George's jaw dropping slightly and his eyebrows arched in wonder. Cook misses only a beat, then clears her throat, nods a greeting and carries on with her work. Just then Alice and Lydia enter through the rear door, Alice's hands filled with kindling from the yard and Lydia carrying an iron cauldron of water for the fire. Alice gives a squeal of appreciation, which draws a sharp glance of admonishment from Cook, and Lydia nearly stumbles in surprise, then excuses herself with a little curtsey of embarrassment. My mistress nods to them all and briefly addresses Cook, making up some nonsense about yesterday's soup and its disagreeable impact on her constitution, which registers like a dark cloud on Cook's visage. We then remove ourselves, leaving Little George bewildered and Alice wide-eyed with appreciation, and Cook predictably out of humour.

From there we proceed to the library where my master is immersed in his books. I have no wish to see him after yesterday, but as it is her desire I have no choice in the matter. He receives us somewhat stiffly, but whether this is due to the previous day's events or the formality of his mother's clothing is not apparent to me. Once again I feel the purse beneath my skirts, where it has been forgotten during the morning's travails, and it suddenly feels over-heavy and awkwardly situated. To my great relief my master does not look at me during the entire conversation, which is just as well as I felt the heat rise in my face as soon as we entered. My mind plays out a fancy in which the purse slips from its position and falls to the floor, the contents spilling out around our feet. I imagine my mistress turning to me with a look of puzzlement upon her painted face, and my mouth goes dry at the thought of it. I cannot seem to stop such thoughts from coming, and I close my eyes and give a little cough to shake the image from my mind. When I open them my mistress is indeed regarding me with a sharply inquiring look.

As we leave the library she turns to face me on the landing. 'Are you unwell?' she asks.

'No, mum. I am quite well,' I say, blushing anew.

'Your colour is excessive,' she declares. 'Perhaps we should send for Lucius to bleed you.'

'That will not be necessary,' I say. She knows that I have been bled not three weeks earlier. Indeed, the entire household undergoes the ritual regularly at her expense, with the exception of Cook who, like my mother, has no time for doctors and their regimens. Lucius bleeds us each in turn in the Great House kitchen, using one of Cook's earthen bowls to catch the spoils. The first time Little George was bled he fainted straight away. Alice, on the other hand, appears to relish the procedure, laughing with delight when her vein is opened, as if the whole thing were part of some sideshow at a country fair. For my own part, I do not look forward to the process but find that once the vein is opened and the blood has started to flow, a curious light-headedness sets in which is not entirely unpleasant. But now I gather my wits about me and steer her towards the stairs.

'Come,' I remind her. 'It is nearly noon.'

Upon our return, the painter awaits us – a fact which embarrasses me but pleases her. He is examining a painting on the wall outside her chamber, a leather case tucked discreetly under one arm. He turns to face us as we enter and nods politely, and immediately I am struck by his youth, for he cannot be more than thirty. His face is clean-shaven, like that of a child, which is unusual these days but not unbecoming in his case, for his skin is smooth and free from scars. His hair is dark and combed straight back from his forehead, falling neatly to his shoulders, and his nose is straight and long. He wears a coarsely woven tunic of deepest green, adorned with only the simplest of collars, black woollen leggings and brown leather shoes which have begun to show their age. But what strikes me most about his appearance are his eyes, for they are a deep and wondrous green, the colour almost luminous in the half-light of the chamber.

My mistress crosses over to his side and nods at the painting on the wall. If he is impressed by her fine dress he does not show it, merely bows to her formally as she indicates the painting with one hand. It is small and rectangular and shows the landscape lying to the west of the house.

'Does it meet with your approval?' she asks with a smile.

'It is very accomplished,' he replies politely.

'My husband commissioned it especially the year before he died. The painter was from Holland, and was among the first to do this sort of work. Perhaps you know of him?'

'No. I have not seen his work before, though I am familiar with the style.'

85

'He was very talented. We had intended for him to complete a set of landscapes of all the land surrounding the house. But he was dissolute, and in the end we were forced to terminate our association with him.' She smiles then, benevolently. The painter says nothing, though I can sense his unease. 'Do you paint landscapes?' she asks.

'No, madam. I only do portraiture.'

'A pity, as I thought to have a study made of the gardens while you were here.' She pauses to see if he will offer his services, but he does not, a fact which surprises me, as most would have been more obliging.

Her smile fades and she bids us follow her inside her chamber. Once inside she lowers herself with some difficulty into a chair and nods for him to be seated.

'I trust your journey was not overtiring,' she says in measured tones.

'It was uneventful,' he replies. His English is fluent but not without an accent. According to my mistress's cousin, he is from Flanders, having come across to England some years earlier to escape religious persecution in his own land.

'You travel unaccompanied?' she inquires.

'I have no need of servants,' he says simply.

'You do not fear our highways then.'

'I have no cause to.'

At this she raises an eyebrow. There has been much talk of danger on the highways of late, of vagabonds and thieves who for a loaf of bread will slit your throat as easily as beg. My mistress cancelled a visit to London only last month for fear of such outlaws. She continues after a moment.

'My cousin speaks very highly of your talents.'

'He is a generous patron,' says the painter. They eye each other for a moment, and I can sense a tension in the air already, as if by his brevity he is somehow taunting her. She clears her throat and smiles a little artfully.

'And your rooms. I hope they are satisfactory?'

'Yes,' he says. 'The light will be useful for my work,' he adds. It is the first comment he has volunteered, and it pleases my mistress.

'You have my lady-in-waiting to thank for that. The tower room was her idea. She thought the aspect would be beneficial.'

He turns to me and for the first time acknowledges my presence with a small nod. I am instantly reminded of my mother's belief that men are only interested in that which furthers their vocation.

'I am grateful,' he says, turning his eyes full upon me. My mistress looks from me to him, then back at me.

'You may go now,' she says somewhat pointedly to me.

And thankfully, I do.

Chapter Eight

W e did not have a looking glass when I was young, as my mother did not countenance their use. But some others in the village did. Dora had one hanging on her wall, and to a child it was a marvellous object to behold, not large but framed in richly dark wood that was carved with leaves and ornamental scrolls all around. The first time she let me gaze upon it I was fearful of my own reflection. Though I had seen my face shimmering in still water, the clarity of my features took my breath away. But in that instant I also felt a sense of disappointment and curtailed possibility, for I was forced to admit the limits of my being. Even as a child I knew immediately that my face could hold only so much in its future, and nothing more; it instantly defined me in a way my own imagination did not.

Dora stood behind me that day and read the disappointment in my face. At once I laid the mirror face down upon my lap, and we both stared at its carved wooden back.

'What is it?' she asked gently.

'I do not wish to see,' I said. She reached across and laid her large, warm hand upon my own. Then she grasped the handle of the mirror and slowly turned it round to face me once again.

'What is it you do not wish to see?' she said. Once again I stared at the girl in the mirror. Her eyes were hurtful.

'That I am plain,' I blurted out. I looked away again, could not bear the sight in front of me. And then she brought her face right next to mine, and lifted my chin to join me in the frame of glass. And simply by her presence my own face improved, as if she'd cast a sympathetic light upon me. She smiled at me in the mirror.

'What part of you is plain?' she asked.

I looked again. My features were small and unre-markable. The things I so admired about her – her walnut-sized eyes and fleshy full lips – I did not find in my own reflection. This seemed to me an indictment of some sort, an outward sign of my inner shortcomings. I had not her spirit or her courage or her strength, and this was written plainly on my face.

'I am not you,' I said finally.

She smiled a little ruefully, and shook her head. 'No.' She laid the mirror down and rose, turning me to face her. 'And one day you will be glad of it,' she said, no longer smiling. And then I saw a trace of something alien in her eyes: a part of her I could not reach. In that instant I longed to be her more than ever.

After that day I did not ask to see the mirror again. Indeed I went some years without so much as a glimpse of my own reflection, until I came to the Great House where the profusion of mirrored panels and vanity glasses meant that I was forced to confront myself at every turn. And though I was relieved to find that my face was not as unpleasant as I'd remembered, it still did not hold the power or the intrigue of hers.

Now, as I cross the great hall towards the kitchen, I am once again reminded of this fact, for the girl in the panel opposite me stares blankly out like some mute farm animal. As if by reflex I look away, avoid her eyes and her damning absence of expression, and disappear into the reassuring warmth of the kitchen.

When I enter, Cook is putting the finishing touches to a pigeon pie, and I can tell from her demeanour that she is still angered by my mistress's visit. She hands me a bowl of onions and a paring knife, and I take my usual seat on a bench near the fire. Little George is there, carefully turning a spitted hare, and the three of us carry on in silence for a time. Gradually Cook's mood lightens, and after a time she begins to hum a little tune under her breath, and even Little George looks relieved.

A knock sounds on the garden door and when Cook opens it my mother stands outside. Cook bids her come inside but my mother refuses, so I rise and go to her. We stand outside the kitchen door, my mother looking around her nervously. She does not like the Great House, indeed has never set foot inside its walls. It is her custom to send messages via Cook whenever she wishes to see me.

'How is the boy?' I ask her.

'He is much improved,' she says with a nod. 'But I must attend a birth across the river. It is a first child, so I may be gone some time,' she explains. She does not want to ask me directly, but I know she wishes me to look in on him in her absence.

'I'll go to him this evening,' I say.

'I'll return as soon as possible,' she says.

'He will be fine,' I say to reassure her. She does not thank me, merely nods and turns away. I stand and watch as she hurries out of the yard, her dark shawl pulled tightly round her shoulders.

It is a sight that echoes my earliest memories. As a child I used to stand at the window and watch her disappear down the lane. She was often called away and almost always at short notice, so that I came to dread the midnight knocks upon our door. When I was still small I would be bundled up in my nightclothes and taken to the house of a neighbour. Goodwife Wimpole was an elderly widow who lived alone in the village and had agreed to harbour me at such times for a small fee. My mother preferred this sort of arrangement to any other, as she had no living relatives and did not wish to be beholden to the women of the village. Goodwife Wimpole was short and grey and hard of hearing, with a thistle of hair upon her chin that reminded me of a goat. Her breath smelled of ale and pickled onions, and her house was small and cold but tidily kept. I had my own makeshift bed in one corner on the floor, with a lumpy straw mattress and an old wool coverlet that smelled of mice. It was there I lay at night listening to the whistling wind and Goodwife Wimpole's whiskered breath, awaiting the return of my mother, who sometimes kept away for days. I did not understand the reason for her absences, nor why I could not accompany her on her journeys. I knew only that birth was a mysterious and difficult process which required the presence of many women, my mother foremost among them.

That babies came from women's bellies I'd been told as soon as I could speak. How they came remained a dark secret which my mother refused to divulge. As I lay in Goodwife Wimpole's cottage, I imagined all sorts of ways in which such a thing might be achieved. But the more I dwelled upon it, the more I decided that the birth of a baby could not occur without the aid of some sorcery or magic. From this I was forced to conclude that my mother was a witch.

One morning after a particularly sleepless night I shared my thoughts with Goodwife Wimpole over breakfast. She blanched and nearly choked upon her bread, then upbraided me severely for speaking heresies. When my mother returned, her face drawn and weary from her own nocturnal labourings, Good-wife Wimpole drew her aside and whispered in her ear. I saw my mother sigh and shake her head, and Good-wife Wimpole crossed herself, before both turned to glower at me. My mother was particularly quiet on the way home, but when we arrived she sat me down at the table and explained as clearly as she could to someone of my age how babies were born. She told me that she did the Lord's bidding, and forbade me ever again to speak of witchcraft to anyone outside our house. The very fact that my mother addressed me in such a serious manner impressed me deeply, though the explanation she gave struck me as highly fantastical indeed, and I was not entirely convinced that what she described could take place without some sort of magic. But I kept such doubts to myself, concluding that if my mother was indeed a witch, then she must have her own reasons for her secrecy.

From the age of eight or nine I pleaded with her to allow me to remain at home, complaining of the draughts on Goodwife Wimpole's floor. My mother lived in fear of draughts and so she finally acquiesced. From then on I was left to tend myself, with only the promise of a neighbour to check upon me from time to time. I relished my new-found freedom and took to wandering about the village after dark, peeping through the cracks of windows at the doings of my neighbours. It was in this way that I came to know of men and women for the first time – of noisy couplings and frenzied tumbling which happened quickly and without warning. The sight initially alarmed me, but soon my reaction turned from fear to fascination and, finally, to amusement, for there was often laughter within, and I somehow imagined myself to be part of the joke.

But it wasn't long before I came to feel excluded. For as long as I could remember, our house had been empty of men. My mother rarely spoke of them, and when she did her comments were terse and vaguely critical. I knew that other children had fathers, but as a child it did not occur to me to ask after my own. Something in my mother's manner cut short even the possibility. Much later, when it became obvious to me that she had not acted independently, the question continued to baffle me. For to this day, I cannot conceive of her together with a man.

My first real brush with men came when I was taken on at the Great House. Indeed for some months I was tongue-tied in their presence, not just that of my master, but the likes of Josias and Rafe as well. Rafe especially, as he was nearest to my age and very forward in his manner. Of course I was not schooled in the ways of women when it came to dealing with men. But it was not long before I perceived that these were numerous and varied. For a time we had a serving girl called Anne to whom I am much indebted for my education. Anne was four years older than I and, owing to her pleasant face and spirited nature, drew much attention from all quarters. She was clever and quick-witted and could be coy or sharp-tongued, depending on her mood. The men of the Great House succumbed to her each in turn, and even my master appeared to alter in her presence, becoming strangely solicitous and even benevolent. Oh, how I marvelled at her powers! That my mother had renounced any claim to this particular sphere of influence puzzled me further. For my own part, while I could not hope to rival Anne's abilities, it struck me that they might one day prove useful.

Anne's final lesson to me, however, was one of prudence. For Anne herself was not, and within a year had fallen pregnant at the hands of a soldier and had run away to London, leaving half the house bereft. To my surprise it was Josias who suffered most, as if some vital part of him had been excised. He was stunned by her absence and went about his duties with the look of an abandoned dog; we even feared for his health for a time. This impressed me even more than Anne's artfulness: that men like Josias, indeed that *any* man could suffer so acutely at the hands of a woman, this was a secret my mother had concealed from me.

Perhaps she'd also kept it hidden from herself.

After my mother's departure I am summoned by my mistress. The painter has retired to his room to prepare his canvases, having completed only a few preliminary sketches, and my mistress is tired and irritable. I help her remove her headdress and cumbersome outer garments and she retires to her bed, saying she will not partake of the midday meal. I leave her to rest and go below to take my supper with the others. The painter has asked to eat alone in his room, and when I arrive Alice and Lydia vie with Cook for the honour of taking up his tray. Cook rolls her eyes at me and hands the tray to Rafe instead, who frowns but acquiesces, as he is remarkably compliant where Cook is involved. Alice pouts and pulls a face as soon as Cook's back is turned, but the matter is soon forgotten.

The presence of a stranger in the Great House often causes ripples of disruption, as if we are a closed circle of stones.

That evening, I hurry along the lane to Long Boy's cottage, anxious to be rid of my new-found wealth. The night is clear and bitter cold and by the time I reach his door my face is numb. But when I enter, the room is empty, though a few charred embers still glow in the fireplace. My first thought is of my mother and a wave of panic sweeps across me as I contemplate her disapproval. Perhaps the boy has gone in search of food, though one glance tells me that my mother has left him with sufficient provisions for some time. Perhaps he has simply gone out to take the night air, as the shroud of his fever still hangs heavy about the room. I stoke the fire and take a seat beside it, thinking to wait for his return, but after nearly an hour I can stand it no longer, and go in search of him.

I walk the length and breadth of the village, stopping to peer into the forest at several points, as I know that he spends much of his time lost among the trees. He has no boyhood friends that I am aware of; always I have seen him on his own, so I am at a loss where to search. Finally, I venture to the alehouse, where I can at least inquire whether anyone has seen him.

As always at this time of the evening, smoke billows

forth from the chimney, and when I push the heavy wooden door open, the warmth and smell of wood smoke buffets me. The room is dark and full of red-nosed men with tankards in their hands, and no one takes much notice of me as I cross the floor. In the back is another room where I go in search of Mary, the tavern owner's daughter, an old friend of mine, now heavy with child. I find her preparing a plate of stewed onions and bacon in the kitchen, and her shiny face lights up when she sees me enter. She is a large, good-natured girl who married young and has done nothing but bear babies since, but she shoulders her burden with ease.

She greets me warmly, then lays a thick-wristed hand upon my arm, telling me to wait while she delivers the plate of food. She disappears into the next room, returning in a moment with a smile upon her lips.

'For the painter,' she says, tossing her head towards the door. 'It seems the Great House left him hungry,' she teases.

'He is here?' I ask, peering through the half-open door. I had not seen him when I entered.

She nods. 'Aye. In the corner. He has hardly uttered two words.'

'He is not the talking sort,' I say, and do not add that this is an understatement. Earlier this evening he declined Cook's offer of food, sending Rafe away with full hands, a fact which did not endear him to either of them. Rafe announced loudly upon his return to the kitchen that he would not play the part of serving girl tomorrow, drawing triumphant looks from Alice and Lydia, and a steely eye from Cook. The painter has been here less than twenty-four hours and already he has angered half the household. I strain to catch a glimpse of him across the room. He is seated alone in a corner by the fire, his head bent over the newly delivered plate of food. When I finally turn back to Mary she gives me a knowing look, which I ignore.

'I've come in search of Long Boy,' I tell her.

'But he is ill with fever,' she says.

I shake my head. 'He has gone.'

She frowns a little. 'We've not seen him here this night.'

'Could you ask about?' I say, nodding towards the other room. She pauses a moment, then lifts her great girth and disappears again. I cross to the door and watch her move about the room, collecting empty tankards and pausing now and then to make inquiries. One by one I see them frown and shake their heads, and she turns to me with a shrug of her shoulders, then moves to fill the empty mugs behind the counter. I remain frozen in the doorway for a moment, unsure what course of action I should take, until I realise the painter is looking at me from across the room. He gives an almost imperceptible nod, then looks down at something in his lap, and I see that he is sketching quickly with coal, his hands flying about the paper. Curious to see, I make my way slowly across the room, but just as I draw near he quickly turns the page, and begins drawing anew. His action seems a little like a reprimand and causes me to halt. I turn and make for the doorway, where I pause to wave goodbye to Mary. But before I can open the door, I am nearly knocked aside by someone entering from without. It is Samuell, Mary's husband, and his broad, weather-beaten face is filled with alarm. Once inside he pauses for breath, his chest heaving and his eyes watery with cold.

'She has gone,' he declares loudly, in a voice thick with panic. 'They've opened the grave and taken her.' For a second there is silence, as it dawns on us who he is speaking of. And in the next moment half the room has risen to its feet, and I find myself swept along in a tide of drunken anger as we all move out of the door.

The graveyard lies on the outskirts of the village, not far from the boundaries of the Great House. Two of the men have managed to grab torches and the light bounces eerily off the frost-laden trees, our feet crunching the frozen earth below us as we hurry along the road. When we draw near we see a small crowd has already gathered around the grave: some yeoman farmers, a few old women who live nearby and must have heard their cries, and standing off to one side, Long Boy. I rush to him and take his arm, and he turns to me with a look of complete bewilderment, as if I am a total stranger.

'Are you all right?' I ask.

He stares at me with a glazed look in his eye, then turns back to the grave, now a shallow hole in the ground. The crude wooden coffin she was buried in lies open at the bottom of the hole, its lid cast to one side, iron nails still jutting from the wood. The men begin to argue among themselves, alcohol fuelling their excitement, and before long their voices rise to shouts and someone throws a punch. A fight ensues between two young farmers, and for a moment no one moves, our attention drawn by the spectacle of violence. Just then Mary arrives at a trot, hands beneath her belly, her breath coming hard. Without a thought she steps right into the fray, shouting at the top of her lungs. Her voice stops them dead, and they pause, chests heaving, regarding her in the midnight air.

'There'll be no more fighting this night,' says Mary with authority. 'Go on home, the lot of you, and put your fists to bed.' The men slowly start to move, bend down to fetch their fallen caps, rub their hands against their faces, and shuffle down the lane.

We stand silently watching them depart through a veil of bitter cold: myself and Long Boy, Mary and Samuell. And then I see the painter, standing several paces away in the shadow of some trees. He must have followed us here, though it surprises me, as I would not have taken him for the curious sort. He takes a step back, disappearing into the darkness, just as Mary speaks.

'Even in death, they cannot let her be,' she says with a sigh.

I turn to Long Boy and he remains motionless, his

eyes fixed to the hole. 'Come,' I tell him gently. 'It is time to return.'

He does not even turn his head, and I shoot a questioning glance at Mary, who shrugs her shoulders slightly in response. Samuell bends down and hoists the cover of the coffin back into place atop the wooden box at the bottom of the hole. He kicks some earth into the hole with his feet, enough to cover the lid loosely. There is something obscene about the sight of the empty box, and when he is done we are all relieved.

'Long Boy, we must go,' I say again, a little more forcefully. And then I take his arm and gently give a tug. He allows me to lead him away, and as our feet hit the path I see that the painter has vanished from his place beneath the trees. Mary must have seen him too, as she glances at the spot and then at me, raising her eyebrows. She and Samuell accompany us back to Long Boy's door, where I turn to them and nod my thanks.

'Do you want me to stay?' Mary asks quietly.

'There is no need,' I tell her. She nods and, taking Samuell's arm, heads off in the direction of the ale-house.

Inside, Long Boy sinks down onto his bed, over-come with exhaustion. He is blue with cold and I move quickly to build up the fire, which has dwindled again in my absence. Then I heat some broth my mother has left and bring it to him in a wooden mug.

'Drink this,' I order, and he does, taking great gulps

of the steaming liquid, just as my mistress does. His eyes wander to the bread on the table and I bring him some, smeared with butter. He tears at it hungrily with his teeth, like a wolf. I sit at the table watching him eat, and as I do I remember the purse of gold stowed beneath my skirts, forgotten in the course of the evening's events. I reach beneath my clothes and retrieve it, open the purse by its drawstring and empty the money onto the table. Long Boy watches me, still chewing, but his face remains a mask of disinterest. I could be chopping vegetables or kneading bread and his reaction would be much the same. I wait until he has finished, then point to the money.

'Long Boy, this is yours,' I say. He looks at me and blinks. 'It is from my master,' I continue. And then, thinking I should offer some explanation, 'It is a gift.' Still there is no reaction from the boy. I lean forward to him, my voice rising a little. 'It is a great deal of money,' I tell him. 'He wishes you to have it.'

'Why?' he says.

'Because we all have need of money,' I reply.

And then he stands and crosses to the middle of the room, a few feet from where I am sitting at the table. He stoops to the floor and fiddles for a moment with a wooden plank, which he prises up and lifts to one side, throwing the loose board down with a clatter. Beneath it is a hole, and in the hole is a sack of hemp cloth which he lifts. It is the size of an infant's skull and he deposits it with a thud on the table in front of me. I pause a moment and he looks at me expectantly, so I lean forward and peer inside, where I see more coins than I can count, enough to make me draw a sharp breath. I look at him.

'This was your mother's?' I ask.

He nods solemnly.

'Where did it come from?'

'From them,' he says simply.

I grope for words. 'She . . . earned this?'

Again, he nods.

I stare at the sack of hemp, incredulous. The men of the village collectively do not have this much money; she must have spent a lifetime amassing it. I cannot help but wonder for what purpose. I glance up at the boy, whose face remains blank. He has no understanding of money and its value; it is merely something to be concealed beneath the floor.

'Does anyone else know of this?' I ask after a moment.

'Only me,' he says, a hint of pride creeping into his voice.

'The men who came here?' I ask.

He shakes his head.

'You are sure?' I press him further.

'Yes,' he says.

I stare at the money for several moments, and cannot help but wonder whether she died for it. I turn to him again. 'Long Boy, I fear you are not safe.'

'Why?' he says.

I nod towards the money. He stares at me with complete incomprehension. He is a simple boy.

I am afraid to leave the money here, but I can think of nowhere else to hide it. Something tells me that he would object if I tried to remove it, not because of its value, but because it was hers. In the end I place my master's purse within the larger sack of hemp and stow both beneath the floor. When the board has been relaid, I am relieved to see that it is indistinguishable from the rest.

'The money will be of use to you,' I tell him. 'It will help you buy food and provisions, until you are old enough to work.'

He frowns then, his eyes narrowing with pain. 'She bought the food,' he says quietly. 'My mother.'

It is the first time I have ever heard him use this word, and a lump rises in my throat. I turn to him and he trembles, then begins to shake all over, uncontrollably. In an instant I move to him, cradle his enormous frame as best I can, comfort him the way a mother does. But no matter how hard I hold him, my arms cannot quell the shaking. I lay him gently in his bed, cover him with quilts, smooth his hair against his head, smooth his trembling shoulders.

'We will buy your food,' I tell him. 'My mother and I.'

I stay with him until he has fallen into deepest slumber, his gangly arms and knees drawn inward, like a child.

That night she visits me in my dreams, and I can see her clearly, for she is standing by the foot of my bed. She wears her death dress, the one she was buried in, and she is as real to me as she ever was in life. She stands by the tiny window in my room, staring out of it into the night, never once glancing in my direction. Slowly I raise myself up, edge closer to her, terrified that she will flee, or simply vanish. Finally she turns to me, and I see her eyes fill and brim with tears. I have never seen her cry before, and the sight of it moves me beyond words. I pause then, see her blink, and as she does, the first tears drop upon her snow-white dress. They fall as blood – and we both stare as great drops of crimson bloom upon her skirts. I gaze at her for several moments, unable to speak. And then she turns and swiftly crosses to the door, pulling it closed behind her, leaving me alone once again.

And then I wake, the moon's rays streaming through my tiny window, a column of unearthly light splitting the floor. The house is deathly still, and I hear only my own laboured breathing, together with the wild beat of my heart. I close my eyes, hoping that sleep will take me quickly, for I do not wish to be alone with the troubled images of my mind.

Chapter Nine

The next morning word has already spread to the Great House that Dora's grave has been robbed. At breakfast there is much speculation among the servants as to the motive, but the sight of her in her death dress remains frozen in my mind, and when I overhear their banter it sickens me. I move to the kitchen so as to avoid their talk, and take only a small draught of ale, drawing disapproving looks from Cook. Afterwards I go to prepare my mistress for her morning sitting with the painter.

Today we are more practised and we complete her transformation in almost half the time. She looks at her reflection in the mirror and sighs a little wistfully.

'What a triumph to be desired even as a corpse,' she says.

Her comment startles me in its boldness. I frown, cannot quell the thought that she has not been taken for this reason, but for some other. Perhaps an even darker one.

'She may yet be found,' I stammer.

My mistress responds with the trace of a knowing smile. 'In the arms of the devil, my dear.'

Just then the painter arrives outside her chamber and she bids him enter. When he does, his eyes dart quickly to mine, then he bows and greets her formally.

'I trust you've passed an easy night?' she inquires.

'I have.'

'And that you've heard the news,' she continues. 'Our little village is not so small as to be completely devoid of entertainment.'

The painter pauses. Her comment is intended to provoke him, a challenge of sorts, though admirably he does not take it up.

'In my country, the thieving of a grave is not thought of in this way,' he says.

My mistress frowns. 'You misunderstand me,' she says coldly. 'It was merely a figure of speech.'

He nods politely. 'Shall we begin?' he says.

'As you wish,' she replies, waving me away with a hand.

Once again I go below to the kitchen, but as I descend the steps leading to the great hall, I meet my master just entering from the cold. He stops short when he sees me, and his face is pinched and white, his hair completely awry. A fit of coughing overcomes him and he reaches out a hand to steady himself against the railing of the stairway. I take a step forward.

'Sir, are you all right?' I ask.

After a moment, the cough subsides, leaving him gasping for breath, which comes in great, raspy draws.

Finally he regains himself and raises his head, his eyes now red and watery.

'I have been to see her,' he says in a voice that is barely more than a whisper. I stare at him, unable to respond. 'The grave,' he says. 'I had to see it for myself.' His eyes are wild with anger now. 'Who would do such a thing?' he says urgently.

'I do not know, sir,' I reply.

He pauses for a moment, regaining his composure. 'How is the boy?' he asks. 'He is recovered?'

I think of Long Boy and his vacant stare. How does one recover from such a thing?

'A little better,' I say slowly. 'He was grateful for your gift,' I add untruthfully.

My master nods, waves one hand, does not wish to speak of it: the dirt of money. 'May God take pity on her soul,' he mumbles, more to himself than me.

I nod and curtsey and he stumbles forward up the stairs with difficulty, grasping the rail as if it is a lifeline.

When I reach the kitchen, Cook hands me a freshly baked scone. 'You must eat,' she says sternly, and I do, for I find that I am suddenly famished. I eat one and then another, watching her movements, until she stops suddenly and turns to me.

'The rising of the dead,' she says, shaking her head slowly. 'It is a sign from God. A warning.' She regards me closely and I stop chewing, my mouth filled with bread. Cook is prone to superstition but her fears are not without cause. She crosses herself, then raises her eyes again to mine.

'It is an omen, an ill one, to be sure,' she says.

I stay with her until the others return. Their presence seems to have a calming effect, and she continues about her work as if no talk has passed between us. After a few minutes I slip away unseen, hoping to check on Long Boy, wondering if my mother has returned. When I reach the cottage, to my great relief I find him there. He seems to know me this morning, though his cheeks are unusually bright and there is an excited spark in his eye. As soon as I enter, he crosses to me eagerly and grabs my hand.

'I have seen her,' he says. 'I have seen her in the night, and she will come for me.'

I take a deep breath, reach a hand to feel his brow. His temperature has risen again, no doubt a result of his night wanderings.

'Your fever has returned. You must lie down.' I take his arm and gently ease him back onto his bed, covering him loosely with the bedclothes. But as I do, something catches my eye beneath his blankets: a small, worn volume bound in cloth of deepest crimson, its threads fraying round the edge. The boy reaches for it and in one smooth motion draws it beneath his pillow, his hand remaining hidden.

'Long Boy, what is this?' I ask, leaning forward.

He watches me distrustfully, then slowly withdraws the volume from beneath the bedclothes.

'Was it your mother's?'

He nods, then opens it, turning it round for me to see. It is a diary of sorts, but not a recent one, for the pages are yellowed with age and the ink has faded over time. I reach a hand out but he flinches.

'The language is some other. Is it your mother's tongue?'

Again he nods, nervously fingering the pages.

'Can you read it?'

My question irritates him, for he shakes his head, snaps the cover shut and slides it back to its hiding place.

'Perhaps we could find someone to read it to you,' I venture.

'It is mine,' he says emphatically.

'Of course. I only thought that it might contain a message for you from your mother.'

'I have seen her,' he says again. 'And she will come for me.' And with that he clutches the diary to his breast and turns his face to the wall.

I have no choice but to leave the volume with him, even though its contents might well shed some light on Dora's death. But even if he were willing to part with it, I do not know that I could find a translator, for to my knowledge there is no one in the village who shared her tongue.

I stoke the fire and prepare some bread and broth, which I leave on the stool by his bed, for he remains turned to the wall.

'You must eat,' I say. 'And rest. I'll come again this evening.' I turn to go but his voice stops me.

'I will wait for her,' he says fervently.

I leave, hoping my mother will return soon, though what she will make of his wild talk I do not know.

Cook has prepared a tray with some refreshment for my mistress and the painter. When I enter her outer chamber I can see that the effort of sitting for him has already left her tired. She rises and excuses herself. I remain behind and offer ale to the painter, who appears oblivious of her fatigue, perhaps wilfully so. He takes the cup of ale but places it to one side so as to carry on with his work. The canvas is covered now with a wash of grey and salmon, and the outline of my mistress can be discerned. After a moment, he lays aside his brush and takes up the cup.

'The woman whose body was taken,' he says after a moment. 'Who was she?' His directness catches me off guard, and for a moment I cannot think how to answer him. It is not an easy question, for she was both a mother and a whore, but these two things do not begin to describe her.

'She lived here,' I say evasively. 'In the village.'

'But she was not from here,' he says. He has clearly overheard talk in the village, probably at the alehouse.

'No. She came across the water many years ago. When I was a child. But she was one of us,' I add quickly.

He smiles a little. 'Is such a thing possible?'

'What do you mean?' I ask.

He pauses, considering his response. 'To be foreign. This is not a skin one loses easily,' he says.

'I do not know.'

'But I do,' he replies. 'How did she die?'

'She fell,' I say. 'It was an accident. She was . . . unlucky.'

He stares at me closely, as if he can read my doubts, and I am forced to look away. He takes up his brush and dabs at the canvas.

'The thieving of bodies . . . does this happen often here?' he asks.

I shake my head slowly. 'No. Never before.'

He raises an eyebrow. 'Was she buried with her possessions?'

'No,' I say, my mind reaching back to the money in the hole beneath her floor.

'Then it is very strange,' he says, with a frown.

'You did not know her,' I say quietly.

'Did you?' he asks.

'We all did.'

'You knew her well?'

I nod my head slowly up and down, imagine she is here listening to my answers, as if it were a test of my loyalty.

'I was very fond of her,' I say finally, and my voice is thin with grief.

The painter frowns. 'I am sorry,' he says quietly. 'I did not know.'

I stare at him. Perhaps I did not either, for we do not feel our thirst until the water has run dry.

At supper that evening there is talk of a search party. A group of men from the village, those that could be spared, spent much of the day combing the forests and fields, but to no avail. No one has a clue to her whereabouts, nor to who has taken her.

'They found nought,' says Rafe, chewing earnestly, his long, black curls bobbing up and down. 'No sign nor trail, though with the ground frozen solid, there'd be none to follow.'

''Tis a heavy load. Whoever it was could not have got far without the help of a horse or pack animal,' says Josias.

'Perhaps there were two of them, or even more,' ventures Alice. There is silence for a moment. Our village is small; how could a group of men engage in such a task without the knowledge of others? Josias frowns and shakes his head.

'Perhaps they came from somewhere else,' he says. 'Outsiders.'

'Aye,' says Rafe. 'It is possible, for she was known throughout the county. I met a man in Chepton once who spoke of her as if she were the Queen.' He pauses, smiles a little, and for a moment we are swallowed by her memory. It is Lydia who finally breaks the silence.

'Perhaps she was not truly dead,' she says tentatively. We raise our heads, regard each other; it is a thought that has passed through all of us like a silver thread. Rafe shrugs and Josias gives a little cough. Indeed, it would not be the first time such a thing has happened. There was a celebrated case not two years earlier in a neighbouring county, of a yeoman farmer who dropped dead ploughing a field. During the course of his own funeral, shouts were heard, much to the amazement of the onlookers, and when the coffin lid was prised open, he sat up and cursed those who'd put him there. The man lived for several months more and then died of drink when he collapsed in a ditch and drowned.

But the great-bellied woman would have needed the strength of an ox to raise herself from below the ground.

'No woman is strong enough for such a task,' says Rafe after a moment. 'No man either.'

Cook enters then, carrying a large bowl of hot broth which she proceeds to serve. She has clearly overheard the talk and her mouth is pressed tightly in a grim line. When she serves out the last bowl she finally speaks.

'We've not seen the last of her,' she says. Then she picks up the serving vessel and disappears into the kitchen, leaving the rest of us wide-eyed.

After supper I slip away to Long Boy's cottage but even as I approach, the smell of fresh-made stew tells me that my mother has returned. When I open the door she is there in the darkness, kneading pastry of some sort. She pauses and looks at me, then raises a finger to her lips, for the boy lies sleeping in his corner bed. Once again, she looks tired and drawn, her face a pool of weary lines.

'When did you return?' I ask.

'This afternoon,' she says. 'I came directly here.'

'How is he?'

'A little feverish, but it does not seem serious,' she says.

'Did he speak?' I ask tentatively.

She looks at me. 'Of her?' she asks, then nods with a sigh. 'I told him she is dead.'

I pause, unsure how to break the news. She reads my mind.

'I have seen Mary,' she says grimly.

'She told you?'

'Aye.' She stares down at the lump of dough. 'May God take pity on her soul,' she adds quietly.

I frown. 'Is it possible she is alive?'

My mother glances up at me with a sharp, scornful look. 'She was dead,' she says flatly. 'I laid her out myself.'

I nod, take a seat beside her. It would be unwise to press her further. She is not given to speculation, sees only the lay of things before her, never what they might have been.

Just then the boy stirs and moans a little in his sleep, and in an instant my mother is at his side, her hand upon his brow. Satisfied, she returns to the table and resumes her kneading.

'How went the birth?' I ask quietly.

She appears not to hear me, carries on with the punch and slap of dough, her jaw rigid.

'Mother,' I say.

She stops and looks at me.

'The baby,' I say. 'How was the birth?'

She pauses for a moment, then returns once again to the dough, flipping it over and reaching for more flour. 'It was still,' she says, her voice as flat as glass.

After a moment she finishes her kneading, placing the dough on the stone hearth to rise. She brushes the flour from her hands.

'Stay with the boy,' she says. 'I have some business to attend to.'

'At this hour?' I ask. 'Can it not wait until morning?'

'It is best done now,' she says with a weary sigh. She puts on her wrap and then crosses to the fireplace, taking up a small iron shovel. 'I won't be long,' she says. I follow her to the door, and just outside she pauses, picking up something lying to one side in the dark.

'Mother?' I say from the doorway.

She turns to me. My eyes drift down to the burden in her hand: a lumpy, dirt-stained sack of cloth.

'Where are you going?'

'To bury the child,' she says.

I look at the cloth, see now that the dark stain upon one side is the colour of dried blood. 'The child is here? Why?'

'I made a promise to the mother . . . to give the baby a proper burial.' She stares at the sack lying heavily in her hand, cannot meet my eyes. 'She had concealed the pregnancy. It was a bastard child. That is all.'

'Where will you go?' I ask.

'To the clearing behind our house. I'll not be seen there.' She is right: the clearing behind our house is well concealed and rarely entered by anyone but ourselves.

'Do you need help?' I ask.

'No,' she says, much to my relief. 'Stay with the boy.' And with that she turns and goes, never once meeting my own bastard gaze.

I close the door and return to the fire, taking up the iron poker and prodding it absently, the bloodstained sack like a stubborn weed planted resolutely in my brain. It is not the first time I have seen her with a sack of blood: the other night in my dream it was much the same. But I know that the real image, the seed, is from another, earlier time.

When I was eight, I secretly followed my mother in the dead of night to Dora's house. Her time had come, and I was determined to unravel the mysteries of my mother's nocturnal life, with or without her permission. And so it was I came to witness my first birth. I followed my mother through the cold, damp night, and perched outside the cottage, peering through a chink in the rough-hewn walls. When we arrived, Dora was already deep within the throes of labour. Her hair was wet and matted, her face an unearthly pink in the glow of the firelight. She wore a simple nightdress, pulled up to reveal the cream of her large thighs, and was crouched by the bed on all fours. I watched as my mother coaxed her onto the bed. She took out a cone-shaped instrument from her bag, one that I had seen her use countless times before in her examinations, and pressed it hard against Dora's abdomen, her face taut with concentration as she listened for the life inside. Dora moaned, and my mother laid a hand upon her shoulder to silence her, and then there was nothing but the spitting of the fire. I watched my mother's face, the look of intensity in her eyes as she strained to hear the life within. After some moments, she shut them tightly, as if to block out everything, and both women remained frozen for what seemed an eternity, Dora scarcely daring to breathe. And then her body jerked with a spasm of pain, and her deep moan split the silence. My mother opened her eyes, and I saw at once the uneasiness they held. Dora rolled over onto her stomach, her haunches slipping to the floor. She stretched her arms across the bed, her face buried in the bedclothes, her upper body heaving with the effort. And then I saw the blood spill forth from between her wide legs.

My mother crouched below her, one hand reaching up into her womb, the look of concentration still heavy upon her face. After a few moments, she removed her arm, now stained with blood, and moved round to face Dora. She took her by the shoulders and spoke directly to her with some force.

'The baby is sideways,' she said. 'There is no sound of life.' Dora panted and blinked and then once again was gripped by pain. My mother released her shoulders and stepped back, and I watched in horror as Dora squatted and pressed down with all her might.

The sounds coming from her throat made my blood run cold: a deep, low growl that was more animal than human. The blood spurted forth anew, and I thought for a moment that she would lose her insides. Instead, a tiny hand appeared between her legs, small and purple and limp. My mother leaned forward again, and grasped her shoulder.

'The baby is dead. I must act quickly. Do you understand?' she said, her voice rising to a near shout.

Dora nodded, blowing and puffing, her eyes wide, and then she threw her head back and roared, the sound reverberating in my ears for days afterwards.

What I saw next I have since tried to forget. I saw my mother pull the arm as far as it would come, and then, taking up a knife, I saw her cleave it from the body. It fell loose onto the floor, like a tiny stick of kindling, then she reached both hands inside the womb and pulled forth a mass of blood and bones and membranes, quickly stuffing all of it into a sack of hemp which she had ready at her feet. After a moment's hesitation, she picked up the arm and dropped it in the sack. She crouched in silence by Dora's side. After another minute, she reached again between her legs, and I thought another child would emerge, but this time it was only blood and membranes. These she stuffed as well into the sack, then bundled it tightly and carried it to the door, depositing it just outside, only a few feet from where I crouched in the darkness.

She returned to Dora, who squatted silently against

the bed, chest heaving, her face turned towards the wall. She had not seen what I had seen, though I have no doubt that she must have known. My mother picked up a cloth and began to wipe the blood from between her legs. Then she eased her up onto the bed. Dora's hair was matted with sweat and when she turned over I saw that her eyes were dull and lifeless. My mother covered her with bedclothes and within moments she had closed her eyes and fallen into sleep.

I looked down at the bloodstained sack lying just outside the door and felt my stomach heave. I stood and backed away from it, turned and ran as fast as my legs would carry me to the cottage. At home I climbed into bed and lay awake shivering in the darkness, my throat bone-dry, my body taut with memory. How had she known the baby was dead? I asked myself over and over. 'I must act quickly,' she had said. Had she sacrificed the child for the mother? And would she have done the same to me in order to save herself?

When she returned, I feigned sleep, scarcely breathing as she readied herself for bed. Once or twice when her back was turned I opened my eyes to look at her. I do not know what I expected, a mark or sign of what had happened, I suppose, but I saw nothing except the usual weariness. In the morning, she went about her business as normal. Finally, when I could stand it no longer, I asked about the baby, and she told me only that it had been born dead. She said nothing of the other: the dangling arm, the bloodstained cleaver, the roar of anguish, the bag of hemp.

Nothing of the things that mattered, the things that plagued my mind.

It was some days before I saw Dora, and when I did she, too, bore no trace of what had gone before. She was splitting logs with an axe in the clearing behind her cottage, and I approached slowly, cautiously, as if she was a creature too delicate to behold. But of course she was not, and as she turned and caught my eye, I saw nothing of her previous anguish. She stopped immediately and laid the axe to rest, extending a hand towards me. I moved slowly, my feet sluggish with the memory.

She must have sensed my unease, for she planted herself upon a thick stump of wood and pulled me onto her knee, her great arms wrapped round me in the kind of embrace my mother never gave. I buried my face in her neck and breathed deeply of her smell: strong and mossy, the damp, wild scent of the forest. She held me there upon her for a long time, rocking me slowly to and fro, and for those few minutes I imagined that it was I, not the other, who had sprung from between her legs.

I never heard another word about that baby. It lived and died within me only.

Chapter Ten

After my mother returns I go in search of Mary at the alehouse. When I enter, the room is full and noisier than usual. Mary is behind the bar filling jugs of ale as fast as she can. She catches my eye and nods towards the kitchen, and I go within, where it is warm, to wait for her. It is some minutes before she is free, and I occupy myself with a joint of mutton that is roasting on the fire, turning it and basting as I go.

'Lord, they drink like fools tonight,' says Mary as she enters, her hands full of empty wooden platters. She deposits them on the table and wipes her hands on a grease-stained apron. 'If you ask me, it is fear that makes them thirsty,' she says.

'Fear,' I say. 'Of what?'

'Of her,' says Mary. 'Or her ghost, whichever be the source of the stories.'

'What stories?' I ask.

'Have you not heard?' I stare at her uncomprehendingly. 'She's been seen,' she says. 'In Chepton town.'

'When? By who?' I ask.

She shrugs. ''Tis only a rumour. But it has them drinking like a herd of horses,' she says with a toss of her head towards the other room.

I frown. Can it be that my mother is wrong?

'He is there as well,' says Mary, interrupting my thoughts. 'Your friend, the painter.' She begins to scour the platters in a bucket. I go to the door and peer into the crowded room. He is alone in the corner by the fire, once again sketching, a tankard of ale by his side.

'Does he speak to anyone?' I ask.

'I did not know he had a voice,' she says with a laugh.

I think again of his questions: they were not asked in idleness. It interests him, this business of Dora's disappearance; *she* interests him, though I do not know why. Truly her allure extends beyond the grave.

'What does he draw?' I ask.

'People,' she says with a shrug. 'Rough sketches only, as far as I could make out.'

'This business of Chepton. When did you hear it?'

'This night only. From some farmers who'd been to market.'

I shake my head. ''Tis nothing but a fancy tale,' I say. Mary picks up a tray and heads for the other room, pausing just before the door. She turns to me with a piercing look.

''Tis a tale *she* might have told,' she says, and disappears behind the door.

The following day my mistress is unwell, and she elects not to sit for the painter. She is disappointed by the process: it does not hold her interest as she thought it would, or perhaps it is his manner which puts her off. She sends a message via Rafe that he will not be needed in her chamber that day, that he may attend her son instead, if he is willing. Then she sends for Lucius, and I am kept occupied with Scripture reading for the remainder of the morning, as we await his arrival.

Eventually she dozes off, much to my relief, for I find I do not have the patience for Scripture these last few days. I take up my sewing, but before I can progress, Alice comes to the door, saying that my master has requested me to attend him in the library.

'For what purpose?' I ask her, a little startled, for he is not in the habit of sending for me.

'I know not,' she says with a sniff. 'Only that the painter is there with him. Perhaps my master desires your good opinion of his likeness,' she says in a teasing voice.

As I make my way towards the library, I can think of only the money and the vial, the two things which tie me to him. When I arrive I find them taking wine, apparently awaiting me. The painter sits to one side, his satchel at his feet, his easel standing to one side, a blank piece of paper pinned to it. My master jumps up nervously as I enter, and ushers me inside with unusual politeness, adding to my growing sense of unease. He thanks me for coming so promptly and offers me a drink, which I decline. Then he gives a little cough and glances over at the painter.

'I have asked the painter to carry out a private commission,' he begins self-consciously. 'It is a portrait of sorts . . . though not my own,' he adds hastily. 'It is my great desire that he undertake a portrait of *her*, and he has kindly agreed to oblige me.' He stops then and regards me hopefully, almost as if he is awaiting my approval. I say nothing, dumb with surprise, and in a moment he turns away, crossing over to the window.

'I thought that using my description, I could assist . . . or enable him to render her likeness, but I find that I have not the facility, nor the heart, for such a task,' he says, looking out upon the grounds. 'Had the body not been taken, it might have been possible . . . if only for a few moments, for him to catch a glimpse . . .' His voice drifts off to almost nothing, then he coughs and clears his throat. 'But such a course is not available to us, so we must seek other avenues. You have proven that both your loyalty and your discretion are beyond question. You knew her well, I believe, and you are capable of fine expression. I would be extremely grateful if you could assist us in our endeavour.' He pauses, awaiting my answer.

I look from him to the painter and back again, speechless.

My silence he interprets as acquiescence, and with a sigh of relief he clasps his hands together. 'I cannot thank you enough,' he says fervently, his relief almost palpable. 'And I shall remain forever in your debt.' He looks from me to the painter, and a taut triangle of silence stretches out between us. Then he limps slowly to the door, where he turns, his hand upon the knob. 'You will have no need of me,' he says. 'My presence here will only serve as a distraction. If you'll excuse me, I shall leave you to your task.' He nods to the painter, then turns back to me. 'I shall go directly to my mother, to make your excuses, so that time will not constrain you,' he says, and then he lurches from the room, and we listen in silence to his laboured gait upon the stair.

I am almost numb with surprise and disbelief. The painter clears his throat, awaiting my response.

'He wishes you to paint her?' I ask finally.

'Yes,' says the painter.

'And I am to . . . describe her?' I cannot keep the incredulity from my voice.

'Yes,' he says, almost matter-of-factly.

'Is such a thing possible?' I ask.

'That depends on you,' he says. 'Your master was not . . . equal to the task.' I stare at him. There is a glimmer of amusement in his eye, as if he secretly relishes my master's incompetence, as if he is taunting me to display my own.

'And you are?' I reply.

'I believe so, yes.'

'But your success depends on mine.'

'In a manner of speaking,' he says with a shrug.

I smile; he cannot say it. 'Then you are in my hands,' I say.

He affirms this with a slight nod. 'I suppose I am.'

I rise and cross to the window, just as my master has done before me. The day is cold and grey and lifeless: the death that is winter. The grass in the orchard is dotted here and there with patches of icy snow, and in the distance a farmer leads an ox along the road, his body doubled over to avoid the icy wind. I try in vain to conjure up her face, and like a wilful child, it eludes me. After a moment I turn back to him.

'The other day, your questions . . . you knew of this before?' I ask.

'Yes,' he says.

'And my mistress?'

'She knows nothing,' he says.

'And if I refuse?'

He shrugs. 'Then he must learn to live without her,' he says, seemingly indifferent. I presume he is not indifferent to his commission.

'Just as the rest of us must do,' I say. We regard each other silently for a moment, and then I turn back to the window, search the fields once again for her face. This time she comes to me in fragments: I see her eyes, and in the next instant her hands, their long slender fingers stretched in front of me. But try as I might, I cannot see the whole. I shake my head from the effort, turn and cross the room to pour myself a glass of wine, which I stand sipping quietly for a moment. I do not for a moment believe that such a thing is possible, that through my memory and my words I can bring her to his canvas. But something in me wants to try.

'How do we proceed?' I say finally.

He regards me for a moment, then reaches down to his case and retrieves a lump of charcoal, the sort I have seen him with at night, when he sketches in the tavern. He reaches for the easel, repositions it closer to him, turning the blank sheet away from me.

'Tell me everything,' he says. 'Everything that you remember. Start at the beginning.'

And so I do.

As I speak, he begins to draw, his hands moving rapidly, fluently across the page. From time to time he reaches for a clean sheet, pinning it on top of the others, and begins to sketch anew. I tell him of my earliest memory: the feel of her drum-tight belly against my brow, the colour of her speckled eyes. I tell him of her stories, and of the light in her face when she told them. I tell him of the others, the ones that came to see her, the look of them as they entered, and the step of their gait when they took their leave. I tell him of the boy, her son, and of his appetite, and of his endless, gaping, loyalty to her. I speak for what seems like hours, but contrary to his request, I do not tell him everything. That is my prerogative; I pick and choose from my memory as one might from a banquet table. I do not speak of the money hidden beneath her floorboards, nor of the tears of blood upon her death dress, nor of the reach of the tiny arm from deep within her. These things I keep to myself, though they come to me frequently, hovering about my mind like moths worrying a flame.

At length I pause, regarding him, and eventually he lifts his eyes from the page.

'What do you draw?' I ask.

'Your words,' he says. 'Your stories. It helps me to concentrate. And to remember.'

'May I see them?' I ask.

'If you wish,' he replies, his eyes meeting mine in a sort of challenge.

But something in me does not wish to see.

'Perhaps later,' I reply.

If he is disappointed, he does not show it.

'Is there more you wish to tell me?' he asks. It is an innocent enough question, but it unsettles me, for I realise suddenly that what I have told him is not the story of her life, but the story of my life with her. And in that instant I am aware that my portion of her life was like a tiny crumb out of the whole – and the idea that I was not privy to it all leaves me with a deep feeling of resentment.

I cannot tell him that I do not mourn her death but the lack of her in my life – a thought which strikes me as unbearably selfish.

The painter peers at me. 'Are you all right?' he asks.

I look around and see that darkness has fallen outside. I feel as if I have been drained of her – and am tired from the effort of remembering. My head has begun to ache, and my throat is parched and sore.

He lays aside his charcoal with a sigh, and I sense that he, too, is tired.

'We will stop now,' he says. 'Tomorrow we will begin in earnest.'

I watch him remove the pages from the easel, wondering what excuse my master has given to his mother. He carefully rolls them up, securing them with a string. Then he removes a blackened cloth from his satchel and wipes the charcoal from his hands.

'I suppose you find us rather curious,' I say.

He lifts his eyebrows and shrugs. 'All people are curious,' he says. He does not even grant us the distinction of oddity.

'These past few days . . . my master has been greatly affected,' I say. 'He is not himself.'

'I envy him,' he says with sudden intensity. 'I envy his devotion.' His eyes have deepened somehow and his cheeks have filled with colour. And then he coughs and looks away, his embarrassment evident. Though I have talked for hours, my words nearly filling up the room, he has said almost nothing, except this last, lone utterance. It has escaped him, like a loose page fallen from a book, and as I watch him cross the room, I can already read his regret.

When he reaches the door it dawns on me that I have forgotten about the portrait in her cottage. 'Meet me at the tavern this evening,' I say. 'There is something I must show you.'

He turns to me and nods, and then he is gone, leaving me to face the falling darkness.

That night I return to Long Boy's house to collect the miniature. As always, my mother is there when I arrive, but she is bone-tired and needs little coercion from me to return home. Long Boy's fever has abated but there is a glassiness in his eyes which I find disconcerting, as if the illness has left a residue behind. He does not speak, merely lies in bed and stares at the wall. I offer him food but for once he declines, though after a time he accepts a cup of warm broth.

I wait until he falls asleep, then remove the miniature from its wooden box and hide it under my kirtle. I hurry along to the alehouse, thinking I will only stay a short while, long enough to meet the painter and show him the portrait. But when I arrive he is not yet there, so I go to the kitchen to await him.

Samuell is on his knees tending the fire when I enter, his face reddened from the heat and his hands covered in ash.

'What news of Chepton?' I ask him straight away.

'I saw no ghosts, if that is your meaning,' he says, standing up and brushing soot from his legs. 'Nor corpses either,' he adds with a smile. I think of his face the other night when he burst into the room: the whiteness of his pallor and the look of fear within his eyes.

'You saw nothing?'

He shakes his head.

'Did you ask about?'

'Aye, and they thought I was well mad,' he says, lifting a heavy iron cauldron onto a hook over the fire.

Just then Mary enters carrying a pail of water.

'Samuell, they need you in the yard,' she says. Samuell nods and goes outside.

'You were right,' she says to me. ''Twas but a tale.'

'And you've heard nothing since?' I ask.

She shakes her head.

'Perhaps it was no more than a practical joke,' I say.

'A poor excuse for poking fun, if you ask me, at the expense of the dead,' she says, pouring water from the pail into the cauldron over the fire.

'Who knows where rumours come from?' I reply. The great-bellied woman claimed that there were fairies in the forest; that they came to us in the dead of night and whispered half-truths in our ears. Perhaps she was right.

I rise and cross to the door, looking to see if the painter has arrived. Mary gives me a piercing look. 'He is later than usual,' she says knowingly. I tell her of the miniature, and of my master's commission. She looks at me askance.

'Why, 'tis morbid beyond belief. And you agreed?' she says, raising her eyebrows in a sceptical arch.

'I had no choice,' I say, not entirely truthfully. 'It was my master's wish.'

'And if he asked you to lie upon his bed, I suppose you'd grant him that as well?'

'I could not see the harm. He is lonely, and misses her terribly.'

'Like half the village,' she says, with a nod to the other room. ''Tis his own fault. He need not be alone.

133

There are many who'd have him, with his wealth and good looks.' She turns and throws me an irreverent grin. 'Let's have a look at it then,' she adds.

I remove the frame from beneath my skirts and open it. For once Mary is serious, her eyes poring over the tiny painting.

'This is a fine thing indeed,' she says with awe, cradling the tiny frame in her calloused palm.

'Do you see the likeness?' I ask.

'If this is all he has to work from, then he will have a job to do,' she says doubtfully.

'It isn't all,' I say, reaching for the portrait and closing the frame.

'I forgot,' she says with a teasing smile. 'He will have you as well, and all your fine words.'

She returns to the other room, and I sit upon the stool to wait. Once again I open the frame to study the face within. The woman is indeed beautiful, more so, perhaps, than Dora, but without the same allure. The mouth is very like, especially in the fullness of the lips, and the eyes are of a similar type, but they are not a match. I will be hard pressed to explain the differences.

The door opens suddenly and he is there, standing behind Mary, who ushers him in and then returns to the other room with a wink. The painter removes his hat and smiles apologetically. 'Forgive me,' he says. 'I was delayed.'

His politeness takes me by surprise and I am at a loss for words. He steps forward, indicating the por-trait in my hands.

'Who is this?' he asks.

I rise and hand it to him. 'I found it in her cottage,' I explain. 'I think it is her mother, for there is some resemblance.'

He studies it intently for a moment, turns the frame over and peers at the signature, then shakes his head in disbelief. 'This painter, I was apprenticed to him for some years before he died. He is from my country and was among the first to do this sort of work,' he says. 'You did not tell me your friend was Flemish.'

'I didn't know,' I say. Dora spoke only rarely of her past, and in the most general terms.

'The woman too,' he says, indicating the miniature.

'You know her?'

'No, but I have seen her likeness before. My teacher had another portrait of her, a full-size one, hidden among some old canvases in his studio. When I asked him who she was, he told me only that the portrait had not pleased her husband, and that in the end his commission had been withheld. I thought it strange at the time, for the portrait was exceptionally well rendered, and the woman herself very beautiful.' He cradles the miniature in the palm of his hand and I feel a sudden stab of envy that I am not the one he speaks of.

'Perhaps there was something between them,' I suggest.

'Perhaps,' says the painter. 'He was a married man, but his real devotion was to his work. Until that time I had no reason to suspect otherwise. Some time later I looked for the portrait and it had disappeared. I never knew whether he destroyed it or removed it to some other place.'

We both stare at the woman in the frame. 'She is indeed very beautiful,' I say.

'The woman's family must have been wealthy for such a painting to be done.'

I think of the money hidden in the cottage: perhaps Dora had not earned it as I'd thought. But something in me resists the idea of her former life, as if she did not come across the water but sprang straight from the sea.

'I know nothing of her family,' I say. 'She never spoke of them.' The strangeness of this strikes me for the first time, for she herself had somehow disavowed her former life.

'You said she has a son,' he says.

I nod. 'In the village.'

'May I see him?' he asks.

I hesitate, think of Long Boy and his glassy stare. But now he sleeps. There can be little harm in seeing him now.

'Come with me,' I tell him.

We walk in silence, the frozen soil hard beneath our soles. As we approach the cottage I grow uneasy, but when we enter I am relieved to find that he is fast asleep. I should not have worried; it is late and he is but a child. His giant frame seems to stretch endlessly across the bed, and I watch as the painter takes in his size, for I have given him no warning of this fact.

'How old is he?' he asks.

'Eleven,' I reply. 'He is big . . . for his age.'

'For any age,' murmurs the painter, moving closer to the bed. 'Still, he has the face of a child,' he says softly. After a few moments he takes out the miniature and compares the sleeping figure of the boy with the portrait.

'Which of them did she more closely resemble?' he asks in hushed tones.

It is not an easy question; she was so much herself. 'The boy,' I say finally, for he is flesh and blood, and the other is no more than pigment, though I do not say this to the painter.

'What of the shape of her face?' he asks.

'Similar to his,' I say. 'But broader in the cheeks.'

He nods. 'And the mouth?'

'More like the portrait.'

He studies it anew. 'And the eyes?' he says after a moment.

I hesitate. This is perhaps the most difficult, for our eyes define us more than any other feature.

'They are similar to both but not a match,' I say finally.

'May I keep this?' He asks, indicating the miniature. 'Only until the portrait is complete,' he adds.

I am unsure. It is not mine to lend, but I have already taken liberties, and Long Boy is unlikely to miss it in his current condition.

'If you wish,' I reply.

He nods and stows it in his pocket. As I watch him, a thought occurs to me, and I move closer to the bedside. 'There is something else,' I say. 'A diary, written in her tongue.'

The painter raises an eyebrow.

'The boy keeps it hidden with him.'

The painter steps forward and we both stand over the sleeping figure. 'On his person?'

'Beneath the bedclothes.'

He watches as I kneel down and delicately slip my hands beneath the blankets. The boy stirs, and I freeze, but after a moment he is still and I continue my search. Slowly, methodically, I work my way around his body, moving from his head down to his feet, but I find nothing.

'It was here the other day,' I say, exasperated.

'Perhaps he has hidden it elsewhere.' We both turn and look around the room. At once the painter's eyes light upon the small wooden chest. He crosses over to it, instinctively running his hands along the side until his fingers release the hidden catch. The lid springs open, and he steps back, his hands falling to his sides.

'How did you know what to do?' I ask.

'I have seen its type before,' he says slowly, as if the memory eludes him. I step forward and reach inside, but the volume is not there. I close the box and we continue searching the room in silence. At length, we are forced to admit defeat, but not before my eyes come to rest on the spot beneath the floor where the money lies hidden. It is the only remaining hiding place – but I do not reveal its existence to the painter, for I cannot know if he is worthy of my trust. The thought unsettles me, and as I turn to him, the boy coughs in his sleep.

'You'd best go,' I say.

'Do you return now to the Great House?' he asks.

I shake my head. 'I must stay. To tend the boy.'

He nods, and his relief is evident. A gaping silence opens up between us, spreading like a fog across the room.

'Until tomorrow then,' he says finally.

I wait several seconds after he has gone, then quickly kneel and lift the wooden plank, reaching down into the hole. But inside my hands find only the skull-shaped sack of coins. And once again, I feel that Dora has slipped away.

Chapter Eleven

The following morning I take my mistress her breakfast and I am shocked by the sight of her. The emetic Lucius administered yesterday has left her greatly weakened, her pallor is pasty, and when she turns to me, I can see that her eyes have difficulty focusing. I stand frozen in the doorway for a moment.

'Who is there?' she calls out to the darkness, for her curtains remain drawn from the night.

'It is only me, mum,' I announce and enter the room, placing the tray on the table by the window. I open the curtains, allowing the morning light to flood in. When I turn back to her, she has lowered her eyes to the bedcover in front of her. She gestures awkwardly towards the curtain with one arm.

'No light. I cannot face the light today.'

'Yes, mum.' I close the curtains once again, leaving only a crack of light to split the room.

'That is better,' she says. 'But it is no use, standing over by the window. I can see almost nothing of you there,' she says with creeping irritation.

'Forgive me, mum,' I say, and move to the side of her bed. She slowly turns her head to face me. 'Will you take breakfast?' I ask. She nods and I pour her a cup of warm ale and place it in her hands. I draw a chair to her bedside and perch upon it while she drinks. She slurps it noisily and with obvious thirst.

'I woke some time ago,' she says, 'but I could not find the bell.'

'I'm sorry. It is here beside you, on the table.'

She turns and looks, surprised to see the bell in its usual place, then shakes her head as if it has appeared by magic.

'You must rest today,' I say.

'It is only that wretched antimony,' she says with a wave of her hand, referring to Lucius and his cure. 'He gave me overmuch. But I shall remain in bed. I gather Edward requires you in the library today.'

I nod uneasily, unsure how to respond. What has he told her?

'I am greatly relieved he has agreed,' she says with a sigh. 'I have never had a proper portrait of him. My husband did not wish to be reminded of his deformity. Nor have it recorded for posterity.' Her voice takes on a brittleness as the past rushes over her. She looks away towards the window, moistens her drying lips, appears to forget that I am there.

I did not know my master's father, only of his fearsome reputation. By all accounts he was a cold-hearted man. It was said that when my master was born his mother burst into tears at the sight of him, and that his father took one look at him and left the room. He was not expected to live and was put out to a wet nurse for the first three years of his life. His family never anticipated his return. When he finally did, it was rumoured his father could scarcely tolerate his presence, and that he never once laid a hand upon the boy, either in fondness or in anger.

My mistress sighs and plucks at the bedclothes. 'Of course, my husband himself was of a delicate constitution,' she says with a wandering look. 'His heart was fatally weakened in a riding accident when he was young, and after that he was forced to lead a retiring life.'

I look at her askance, for this version of him does not accord with the others I have heard.

'A large family would have proved too much for him, you see. Particularly after the shock of Edward's birth. I would have liked another child, a daughter perhaps, but his physicians warned me that the stress of even . . . normal conjugal life would prove too great a risk.'

Her bluntness startles me, and I look away in embarrassment, but she appears not to notice. I rise and fill her cup.

'But he is dead now,' she continues. 'And I am mistress. And a portrait can be rendered to suit one's tastes, provided the painter is compliant.' She takes a sip of ale. 'Though I fear this one is not,' she adds. 'I have written to my cousin the Earl to say that I find the painter's attitude peculiar for someone of his station, though I took pains to conceal my displeasure, as I did not wish to give offence. He is an earl, after all, and may yet be of use to us. But I do find his painter most unpleasant. It is a wonder you can tolerate his presence all day long.'

She looks at me then, and I smile and keep my silence, for I cannot believe that she would approve of my involvement, and yet she appears to.

'I know Edward is uneasy at the idea of a portrait. It must be a great comfort to him to have you read while he sits,' she continues. 'And I am certain I shall be well pleased with the result. The painter may be arrogant but he is not without talent, if I am to believe my cousin.'

I smile again, this time with relief, and wonder if Edward's falsehoods to his mother come as easily as my own.

'At any rate, do not trouble yourself over my welfare,' she continues. 'Cook has promised to attend me, and Lucius will look in on me later this morning, though if he tries to administer any more of that wretched antimony, I shall have him forcibly removed.' She squints at me then, scrutinising my dress, a simple one of china-blue muslin with a deep, square neckline. 'Take pains to keep your throat covered,' she says, indicating my bare neckline. 'Or you shall lose your voice.'

'Yes, mum,' I reply. And willingly I take my leave.

I hurry along to the library and when I arrive the painter is already there. He has a sheaf of paper before him and has been making sketches. The miniature lies open on a table to one side, within his view. When I enter he stops sketching and stands, greeting me with a polite nod. Once again his manner is formal, and I feel myself stiffen in response. His eyes flicker briefly across my dress – the low neckline, the gathered waist – and I realise in an instant that I have dressed for his benefit, a fact which embarrasses me now that I am here. He has drawn a chair up next to where he works and indicates that I should be seated.

'Today you shall watch,' he says. 'And shape my lines with your memory.'

I stand frozen for a moment, my mind a blank, remember his caustic remarks about my master being unequal to the task.

He nods again at the chair, awaiting me. 'May we begin?' he asks pointedly.

'Yes of course,' I stammer, and take my seat next to him.

'I've made some sketches based on what we saw last night,' he explains in an efficient tone. 'I should like first of all to render the outline of her face. Once we have achieved this, we will find it easier to continue.' He spreads out three sheets in front of me, upon each of which he has made a sketch. I recognise at once the boy's face on one of them and marvel at his memory. The other two are variations on the first.

'You said the cheekbones were wider, though I was not sure if you meant this,' he indicates the second, 'or this. Or perhaps something different altogether.'

I study the drawings for a time. 'It is more like this one,' I say finally, pointing to the third. 'But the forehead should be broader as well.' He picks up his charcoal and begins to sketch anew, this time incorporating the changes I've suggested.

'Like this?' he asks.

I hesitate. 'I believe so, yes.' In truth I am not certain.

'Once we add the features it will become clearer,' he says, sensing my doubt. 'The eyes, you said, are similar to the boy's. I take this to mean that they are large and fairly round and deeply set, like so.' He sketches while I watch, and suddenly the boy's eyes are there, staring out at me from the page.

'Hers were not so round,' I say slowly. 'And her eyebrows were heavier.' He adjusts the sketch and the transformation begins. At length I see the shadow of her eyes appear before me.

'Like this?' he asks.

'It is very like,' I say, my voice barely above a whisper. It is as if he raises her from the dead in my presence, and the fact unnerves me slightly. He stops and I feel his gaze upon me, but I find it hard to tear my eyes away from those on the page. When I do, he is staring at me so intently that I blush and look away.

'You are certain?' he asks.

'Yes,' I reply.

'Good.'

We continue like this for a time. He questions me closely, probing and pushing me towards a response.

Twice he starts anew, believing he cannot correct his errors, and each time my heart quickens with regret to see him tear the sheet and throw it to the floor, as if I am losing her all over again. But he is tireless, recreating her time and again, adjusting, altering, shifting. Eventually he stops and reaches for the cloth to wipe the charcoal from his hands.

'We will stop here,' he says. 'Sometimes if you look too long upon a thing, it becomes difficult to see. Tomorrow the errors will be more apparent.'

I nod, feel a pang of disappointment that we will not complete the likeness now, but he is right, as I can feel that I am beginning to lose my focus.

'Perhaps we could have a drink?' he asks.

'Yes of course,' I say, rising to my feet. I leave the room and once outside I feel the sweat trickle down my sides – my face feels hot and my throat dry. I hurry along to the kitchen and am relieved to see that only Cook is present, for I do not wish to confront the jibes of Alice, Rafe or Lydia. But even Cook is curious as to my prolonged presence in the library.

'You've been long up there,' she says.

'The master wishes me to assist with the portrait,' I say.

She raises an eyebrow. 'Take care he does not steal your soul,' she says.

I pause and smile at her. Cook is old-fashioned in her thinking, believes that portraits have the power to diminish one's essence.

'You need not worry,' I tell her with a laugh. 'It is not me he paints.'

She looks right at me. 'Aye,' she says. 'I know.'

Back in the library I pour a glass of wine for us both. Now that we are no longer working, I suddenly feel as if I am trespassing in my master's place. And, when the painter and I do not speak of *her*, the awkwardness between us returns just as quickly as it did the previous evening. It is as if she is a bridge between us all – my master, the painter and myself – joining us together in her absence. We drink in silence for a minute, until the quiet becomes oppressive. Then the painter stands and crosses to the window.

'Why did you leave your country?' I ask.

'I had no choice,' he says, turning back to face me. 'Had I remained, I would have almost certainly been killed.' He says this easily, as if the fact of it does not unsettle him. There have been many killed on the Continent for their beliefs these past few years, and it is said that the streets of London are lined with those fleeing religious persecution in their homelands.

'So you did not wish to leave?' I ask.

'I would have preferred a choice,' he replies. 'Perhaps I might have left anyway. There are many opportunities here for someone of my profession.'

'Where did you learn to paint?'

'My father was a cobbler. From the age of seven I worked as his assistant. I was clever with my fingers and before long I could stitch a sole in half his time.

Then, when I was eleven, my parents were both killed in a fire. I was sent to an orphanage, where I remained some months, until I was taken on as an apprentice by a goldsmith. It was he who taught me the art of limning, and how to use a brush and pen. After a year, he sent me to a distant relative, the portrait painter I spoke of. I remained with him for five years, until he died when I was seventeen. By then I was skilled enough to make my own way.'

'I am sorry about your family,' I say. He turns back to the frozen glass in front of him.

'It was a long time ago,' he says quietly.

I think of Long Boy, also an orphan at the age of eleven. Where will he be in twenty years' time?

'You were fortunate to learn a trade,' I say.

'It was not luck but fate,' he says without hesitation. 'As a child, I was sensitive to light. Sunlight nearly blinded me with its brightness, and colours were so strong as to be almost overwhelming. As I grew older, it became easier. I became more tolerant, and I learned to make use of my eyes and their sensitivity, until eventually it seemed more a gift than a burden.'

He turns and fixes his gaze on me, and I cannot help but wonder what he sees. He envies my master his devotion, but I envy him his conviction. Like Dora, he is certain of his place within the world. I have never known such certainty, and I cannot help but wonder for what purpose I was constructed. The painter notices my distraction.

'What is it?' he asks.

Before I can reply my master knocks and enters, his face brimming with expectancy. 'How goes your task?' he asks.

'We've made much progress today,' says the painter, and looks towards me for confirmation. I smile and nod, though in truth I do not share his confidence.

'Excellent,' says my master, and he shifts back and forth a little nervously. 'Might it be possible . . . for me to see?'

'We are not ready,' says the painter quickly. 'That is, the painting is not ready.' I cannot help but look at him, but he avoids my eyes.

'Yes of course,' says my master almost deferentially. 'Forgive my interruption. I am pleased at the news.' And with that he bows to us both, and departs. Once he is gone I smile at the ease with which the painter handles him.

'Do you always treat your patrons in such a way?'

He shrugs, the corners of his mouth turning up in a half-smile. 'I treat everyone the same,' he says. 'Is this not right?' And then he looks at me intently. And I wonder whether I would have him treat me any differently from the rest.

'Of course it is,' I say. 'How long will you remain here?'

'As long as my presence is required,' he replies.

'And then?'

'Another commission, God willing.'

'You do not fear such . . . uncertainty?' I grope for

this last word, but what really strikes me is the rootlessness of his life. He is tied to nothing but his talent, and I do not know whether I envy or pity him for this.

'I have always found my way,' he says.

'But you have no home to return to?' I ask.

He looks around at the walls of the Great House, then back at me. 'None such as this,' he says, with a thin smile. His meaning is evident, only half-cloaked in politeness.

I look around the room at the book-lined walls, heavy velvet drapes and thick, studded floors. What home is this for me? Where am I lodged within these walls? I turn back to him and his expression has suddenly softened.

'You are fortunate,' he says quietly.

But I do not believe him.

A few minutes later I take the tray down to the kitchen, and as I enter I see Mary at the door. Cook turns to me, her face ashen, and Mary steps forward with urgency.

'She's been found,' says Mary breathlessly, her hands cradling her massive belly. 'In a cave by the river. Some children found her there this morning.'

In my mind I see the children playing by the river – see their stricken faces.

'Has anyone gone to fetch her?' I ask.

'Samuell and John and a few of the others,' she says. 'They've yet to return.'

'What of the boy?' I ask. 'Does he know?'

'Not yet. I came straight here. I thought it best that you . . .'

I nod. 'What will they do with her?'

'Bring her to the barn at the alehouse for now. Tomorrow the magistrate can decide.' She stands in the doorway, her face twitching with alarm.

'What is it?' I ask.

She looks from me to Cook, and takes a deep breath. 'They've cut her open,' she says. 'The children said her belly had been split like a melon.'

'She was with child,' I murmur.

Mary shakes her head. 'There was no mention of a child,' she says.

Cook crosses herself. 'Lord help us,' she says under her breath. ''Tis the devil's work.' Mary and I stare at each other intently.

'I must get back,' she says finally.

'I'll come with you,' I say, and go to get my cloak.

We hurry along to the alehouse, and by the time we arrive, there is already a small crowd of people awaiting the party's return. Mary tells them fiercely to buy a drink or be gone. A few scatter but most shuffle inside and for the next few minutes she is kept busy at the taps, filling tankards of ale. I hover in the kitchen, peering out of the back door from time to time. At length I hear the men return and we file into the yard to meet them. Samuell nods grimly to Mary and myself. They have strapped the body to a sledge and covered it entirely with a horse blanket. Samuell tells the men to take the body inside the barn, then turns back to the small crowd which has flooded the yard with curiosity.

'You can all go back inside,' he says. 'There'll be no public showing.' The crowd hesitates, then one young farmer steps forward.

'What news do you bring, Samuell?'

'Naught,' he replies brusquely. ''Tis but a corpse. And one you've seen before. So be gone with you.' He waits while the crowd slowly disperses, then turns back to Mary and me. Mary lays a hand on his arm.

'It's her then, is it?' she says quietly.

'Aye,' he replies with a tired sigh. He lowers his voice. 'And she's a bloody mess.'

'They cut her?'

He looks around a little furtively before continuing, 'It was as they said . . . split her belly open.'

'Was there any sign of a baby within?' I ask.

He shakes his head. 'If she was with child, then they've taken it, for she's been gutted like a fish.'

At that moment I am overcome with nausea and must turn aside. Mary lays a hand upon my shoulder and gently steers me back into the kitchen, where she forces me to sit. She pours a mug of ale from a jug on the table and places it in my hands.

'Who would do such a thing?' I ask. 'I mean . . . for what purpose?' Mary shakes her head slowly from side to side. 'I thought . . . it was *her* they wanted. But now it seems as if it was the child.'

'Maybe the father,' she suggests.

'But why? Why not let her take it to the grave? There is no sense in it.'

'Drink,' she orders, then watches to make sure I do. 'Perhaps Cook was right,' she says finally. 'Perhaps it *was* the devil's work.'

I think of my mother, and Long Boy in his bed. If I do not go to them, someone else will, for news travels quickly in our little village.

'I must go,' I say, taking up my cloak. Samuell enters and I turn to him. 'What will you do with her?' I ask.

'Keep her under lock and key tonight. The magistrate will come tomorrow.'

I nod, start to take my leave, when another thought occurs to me: the painter and his commission.

'Samuell,' I say slowly. 'How is her face?' He looks at me strangely. 'I mean . . . is it the same?'

'It was untouched,' he says a little suspiciously. 'Why?'

Mary and I exchange glances, and in an instant she reads my mind.

'The boy may wish to see her,' I say, not entirely untruthfully.

Samuell nods, and I slip out of the door, avoiding Mary's disapproving gaze.

When I arrive, my mother and the boy are at the table eating supper. It is as cosy a scene as one could wish for, and in that instant I am sorry she was ever found. They both look up as I enter, and I smile a little nervously, tell Long Boy he is looking well. He nods

154

and continues eating, and I ask my mother to come outside so I may have a word in private. She hesitates, then dons her cloak, following me out of the door.

'What is it?' she says, still chewing. I tell her the news, and as I do the colour slowly drains from her face. When I tell her the baby has been taken, she reaches out a hand to grab my arm, just as she did at the funeral, just as she did the day Dora first came to us all those years ago. After a moment, she turns and looks into the cottage.

'The boy should not be told,' she says decisively. 'He is better today, but the news could set him back again.'

'It is for you to decide,' I say.

'Where is the body?' she asks.

'At the alehouse.'

'Will she be given a proper burial?'

'I do not know,' I say. My mother nods and slowly walks back to the cottage.

'Are you all right?' I ask. But she does not hear me, and in a second she has disappeared behind the door.

Chapter Twelve

Dusk has fallen when I finally return to the Great House. I go at once to check upon my mistress, hoping I will not have been missed, but I need not have worried. I find her dozing in her chamber, her thin grey hair matted against her skull, her parched lips slightly parted in sleep. Her breath comes in short whistles, and when I lean over her to rearrange the bedclothes, I can smell the bile in her blood. The noisome odour shocks me, for it strikes me as the very essence of decay. Despite the smell I lean in more closely, and with alarm I see that the tip of her tongue is blackened by the disease that seems to have lodged within her. For the first time I am frightened on her behalf, for her condition seems less the result of Lucius than some other, greater evil. Her favourite volume of Scripture lies open on the bedside table, and its presence seems almost to mock her. I cannot help but wonder what good are holy words in the face of such devastation, a thought she herself would find heretical in the extreme. I stay and watch her sleep until I can no longer bear the sight or smell, then I steal out of the room like a thief, taking my youth with me.

I hurry quickly to the tower in search of the painter. Dora's corpse may be buried again tomorrow; if he has any hope of seeing her it must be tonight. When I reach his room, the door is closed and I listen for a moment before knocking. But before I have a chance to do so, the door opens and he is standing there, as if he has been waiting for my arrival. I jump back, startled, and he smiles at me.

'Were you spying on me?' he says with obvious amusement.

'I was just about to knock,' I stammer, for he flusters me with his half-smile.

'By all means, come in,' he says, and stands aside for me to enter. I see now that he is wearing his cloak and hat, and his gloves are in his hand.

'You were on your way out,' I say apologetically.

He shrugs. 'It can wait,' he says.

I step into his room a little hesitantly, see his drawings stacked in piles upon the table, his leather satchel upon the floor.

'I'm afraid I have no refreshment to offer you,' he says. I flush, embarrassed at the suggestion that I have come to call.

'She's been found,' I say. 'Her body.'

'Where?' he asks.

'In some caves, not far from where she died.'

'Will it be possible to see her?'

I nod. 'Tonight. Tomorrow they will decide what to do with her.'

He indicates the door. 'Now?' he says.

I shake my head. 'Later. Meet me at the alehouse. She is under lock and key there, and I must contrive a way.'

He removes his hat, runs a hand through his hair, then fixes me with his knowing half-smile. 'You take your duties seriously,' he says, the ring of challenge in his voice.

I look around the room before responding. 'I do not wish to fail.'

'I never thought you would,' he replies, and for a moment our eyes are locked together. It is he who eventually breaks the hold. He gestures to the library below us. 'Does your master know of this?'

I consider this; it is only a matter of time before my master hears the news.

'No,' I say. 'But I shall tell him.'

As usual I find him buried in his books. When I enter, he rises swiftly to his feet and smiles. 'Come in,' he says more politely than usual. It seems my new-found role has altered me in his eyes.

'I have news,' I say. 'Of her.' His face blanches, then he limps round to the front of his desk, as if he can somehow bring her nearer by closing the gap between us.

'Yes?' he says anxiously.

'Her body has been found,' I say. 'In a cave by the

river.' He blinks several times, does not seem to take this in. Did he think she was alive? Finally, he looks down at the volume in his hands.

'It is a great relief,' he says, his voice hollow.

I tell him of the children and the cave, and of her removal to the alehouse. But I cannot bring myself to tell him of the injury to her womb. He slowly shuffles back to his chair and sits down heavily.

'The painter would like to see the body,' I say. 'It would help him greatly.'

'Yes of course,' he murmurs. 'He must see.'

'I shall take him to her this evening, for they will likely bury her again tomorrow.'

'So soon?' he asks, as if he will be losing her all over again.

'I do not know, sir.'

He sits in silence for a moment. 'I should like to look upon her one last time,' he says at last.

I hesitate. It will be difficult enough without him. And yet he is my master. I think of Mary and her chiding words about my willingness. And then I think of the painter, and the sureness with which he handled him.

'It would prove . . . difficult,' I say delicately. 'She is under lock and key, and your presence would almost certainly arouse suspicion.'

His face falls. I refer to his title and stature within the village, but of course he thinks only of his disfig-urement.

'Yes of course,' he says.

'And she may be altered,' I add.

He stares at me for several moments, swallows, and looks away. This last is too much for him.

'Thank you for coming,' he says quietly. And I understand that I should go.

By suppertime, the news has already reached the others, and much has been made of the cut to her womb. The fact that she was pregnant and the baby has been stolen is now common knowledge, and I wonder how much time will elapse before my master learns of it. Or the boy, for surely time will expose all secrets, despite my mother's efforts to protect him.

''Tis a foul thing indeed,' says Josias, shaking his head. 'An act of wickedness beyond belief.' He and Lydia appear truly shocked by this latest episode, while the others seem merely titillated.

'Perhaps this time they'll chain her to the casket,' offers Rafe.

'Perhaps this time there'll be no need,' I say, then instantly regret it, for now all eyes are immediately upon me. Rafe continues chewing slowly.

'So it was the bairn they wanted,' he says after a moment.

They all turn to me and I shrug. 'I do not know,' I say.

'It is possible. Perhaps it was the devil's child,' he says, and I am instantly reminded of Dora's warning to my mother. I stare at my food, determined to say nothing more.

'Aye, there could be sorcery involved,' says Lydia.

'I've heard tales of witches using babies of the dead,' Alice adds excitedly.

'And casting spells upon the womb,' says Lydia.

I raise my eyes and see their flushed faces nod in unison. I cannot bear to hear more, so I quickly finish my food and return to the kitchen, where Cook is busy with a pot of soup. I have not seen her since this afternoon.

'There is trouble about,' she says, fixing me with a knowing look.

I lay a hand upon her arm to reassure her. 'It is past,' I say firmly.

She shakes her head slowly from side to side. 'This is not the end of it,' she says.

I delay some hours before going to the alehouse, waiting in my room until the time is right. When I arrive, the painter is already there in the corner by the fire, an empty tankard by his side. His face is flushed from the heat and his eyes are bright with anticipation, and I cannot help but wonder whether it is the prospect of seeing me or her which brings the sparkle to his eye. I take a seat opposite him.

'I thought perhaps you'd changed your mind,' he says.

'I'm sorry,' I reply, lowering my voice. 'I only wished to wait until there were fewer people about.' He nods and I glance nervously around the room. A dozen hardy drinkers surround us, but alcohol has dimmed their wits and they take little notice. The sheaf of drawing paper lies in front of him, together with a few lumps of charcoal.

'You've been drawing.'

He smiles and shrugs. 'It passes the time.'

'You do not tire of it?'

'Not really,' he says. 'I do it without thinking.' He looks down at his hands, spans his long, slender fingers across the wooden table. 'What my eyes see, my hands need to recreate . . . the urge to draw is part of me.' He smiles at me, then adds, 'Perhaps they cannot bear to be idle.' I think at once of my mother; they share this need for constant occupation. What do they fear in stillness?

I indicate the sketches. 'May I see?' I ask.

He nods and I take up the sheaf of papers and leaf through them. The sketches are rough and quickly rendered, but they are hauntingly lifelike. He has made several and each time the faces are shown in great detail, but the rest is hastily filled in. I glance around the room, identifying each of his subjects in turn: old men, mostly, their expressions marred by drink. But he has captured them on paper, frozen them in time.

'These are very fine,' I say.

'They are only sketches.'

'But they are very like.'

'I draw what I see.'

'And you draw only people?'

'They are all that interests me. Flesh and blood . . .

and bones. And what happens when these things are brought together – the endless possibilities. But always what I seek to render is not the surface, but the life within. It is like a game. One must find the clues in the arch of a brow, or the set of the jaw, or the shadow beneath the eye. This, for me, is the challenge. I have no interest in emblems or allegory. The truth is there in front of us, we must only learn to see it.'

He speaks with great intensity, and as he does I continue to flip through the portraits. When I get to the final page I catch my breath, for there is Mary upon the paper. He has caught it all – the laugh within her eyes and the generosity of her expression. I stare at the sketch and then suddenly, disconcertingly, I hear her laugh. When I raise my head, Mary is standing over us, her face brimming with delight at the sight of the drawing.

'Why, 'tis a mighty chin upon that lass!' she says teasingly. 'Did she charge you for her service?'

The painter smiles and shakes his head. 'She was very generous, and agreed to sit in return for a portrait,' he replies, and with that he tears the paper loose from the sheaf and hands it to her. For once Mary is struck dumb, but she is obviously pleased with the portrait.

'You are very kind,' she murmurs.

'And you have been very attentive in your service,' he replies with a smile.

Mary finally tears her eyes from the portrait and lays a hand upon his shoulder. 'That is because you are the only man worth gazing twice upon within the room!' She throws back her head with a laugh, and the painter flushes. She holds the drawing up next to her face. 'I must find Samuell. Perhaps he'll prefer the new one to the old, for she is quieter and less likely to abuse him!' She spies Samuell through the doorway then and disappears after him, waving the portrait over her head like a banner. The painter looks at me and gives an embarrassed shrug of his shoulders.

'I know no one in this place,' he says, by way of explanation. 'And she has always had a kind word for me.' For the first time it occurs to me that his life must be a lonely one indeed. I slide the pages back across to him and he stows them in his satchel.

'You did not have to help me,' he says quietly. His honesty startles me. I feel the heat from the fire speckle my face, feel it too within me, rising slowly from my depths.

'I wanted to,' I reply.

He nods then, just barely.

A group of old men in the corner begin to sing, their voices low and thick with drink. The painter and I both turn our heads to watch, and while I see them clearly enough in the half-light of the fire, their voices come to me as if through water. After a moment I feel his eyes upon me, and I turn back to meet his gaze, quiet and expectant, unwavering. For a moment, it unnerves me. What does he want?

And then I remember the corpse outside.

'Wait here,' I tell him, and I rise and go in search of Mary.

I find her in the kitchen scouring platters, her face still flushed with pleasure. Samuell holds the portrait up admiringly.

'Your friend is a magician,' he says.

'He is a painter, Samuell. And he is not my friend,' I reply self-consciously.

Samuell smiles somewhat archly. 'Tell him I should like my own portrait done.'

'You can tell him yourself,' I say.

'Perhaps I will,' he says, picking up the jug and disappearing into the other room. I am relieved when he goes, as I wish to speak to Mary alone.

'I need your help,' I say.

She looks at me and in an instant divines my purpose. She shakes her head a little ruefully.

'We'll not be long,' I say. 'And no one need know.'

She eyes me steadily, wipes her hands upon her apron. 'Samuell will skin me if he learns,' she says, but I can see from the glint in her eye that she is not unwilling. She reaches under her kirtle and takes out an iron ring, upon which hang two keys. 'For whom do you do this?' she asks. 'Your master? Or him?' She nods towards the other room.

'For neither,' I say.

'You cannot think that *she* would want it,' she says.

'I have no cause to think she wouldn't,' I reply.

'Perhaps she would be flattered,' she says with a smile. 'I was.' She hands me the ring. 'It is the larger of the two. But take care not to disturb her,' she adds warily.

I give her hand a squeeze of thanks and take the key.

We fumble in the darkness at the stable door, the chill reaching down our necks like a cold hand. The padlock is old and rusted, and the key unwilling in the lock. I struggle with it for a minute, and then the painter steps forward until he is right behind me, and I feel his hand on mine. But instead of taking the key from me, he merely guides my hand with his own, slowly working the key in its place until the padlock springs open. For a moment we stand there, our hands still joined in mid-air, the key held tightly in my fingers. And then he takes a step backwards, releasing me.

When I remove the padlock the stable door swings inward of its own accord. We peer inside for a moment, can see almost nothing in the darkness. I have brought a flint and taper from the Great House, and we move inside and bar the door before attempting to light it. Again my hands fumble in the darkness. I feel them tremble slightly as I try to light the taper, and am grateful that he cannot see. This time he waits patiently by my side, does not interfere. And when I finally succeed, I raise the taper with relief. We pause, scan the room in the feeble light, and see the corpse laid out upon its sledge in the corner, as if it is awaiting us. We cross over to it and I hold the taper while the painter unties the rope which binds the blanket to her body. When this is done he turns to me uncertainly. I nod and he slowly draws the blanket from her body. I move closer so that the taper casts a neat circle of light down upon her.

But I am not prepared for her death face, for it is cold and rigid like the mask of a player, her features are grotesque and the life has long since vanished. I stare at her, thinking of the woman I have spent the past few days remembering, the woman locked within my mind. For she is no more here in front of me now than she was this morning in my master's library.

I turn to the painter and he stands immobile in the half-light, his eyes stunned. Perhaps he, too, was not ready to face death.

'Are you all right?' I ask.

He nods slowly, then moves a step closer to the body. 'Please . . . the taper,' he says in a whisper-thin voice. I hand it to him and he holds it out at different angles, so that the light catches her face. At length he hands it back to me and pulls the sheaf of paper from his satchel, together with a lump of charcoal. He sketches quickly, purposefully, and I can barely make out his impression in the darkness. As I watch, the cold seeps into me, just as death has clenched her in its grip.

After a time he finishes, quickly stowing the sheaf of paper in his satchel. He turns to me and reaches out a hand towards the taper, but as he does so a gust of wind enters through the cracks in the wall and chokes the flame, leaving us in total darkness. I gasp and the taper drops from my hand, and then there is nothing but the sound of our breaths intertwined in the blackness. I feel his hand take mine.

'I am here,' he says quietly.

His voice floats across the space, does not come or go but hovers all around us. And then he steps forward until his body is just next to mine, and I can sense the smell of him, and feel the warmth of his flesh. I turn my face until it is only a fraction from his own, then feel his lips brush lightly against my forehead. I raise my chin to find him in the darkness, can think of nothing but finding it: the warm, dark centre that is him. And then I feel his mouth on mine and I am swimming in his skin, until suddenly, unwillingly, I hear the scrabble of the door and see a thin shaft of light reach across to where we stand.

I turn and trace it back unto its source: a beacon in my mother's hand.

In one quick movement the painter and I separate, and we are suddenly two strangers in a room with a corpse.

My mother stares at us from the open door, her eyes like pinpricks of anger. Her face shimmers eerily in the half-light of the beacon in her hand. I see a movement behind her and Samuell steps forward from the shadow of the doorway, his expression confused.

'How came you here?' he asks sharply.

'It is my fault,' I say quickly. 'I wanted to look upon her one last time.'

Samuell looks from me to the painter and back

again. I keep my eyes upon his face, avoid my mother's scrutiny.

'What of him?' he asks after a moment. I hesitate before replying, but the painter intervenes.

'I asked to see,' he says quickly. 'The dead are of interest to one of my trade.'

'She is not some curiosity at the fair,' says Samuell.

'Forgive me,' says the painter.

'You can ask the Lord's forgiveness. It is not mine to give,' says Samuell. Just then a man's voice shouts for him in the yard. He hesitates, then looks at me.

'We'll not be long,' I say. He turns and goes out, leaving me to face her in the flickering light.

'Mother,' I say after a moment. 'Are you all right?'

She nods then, slowly. 'I've come to pay my last respects,' she says finally. She looks only at me, does not acknowledge the painter's presence.

'The boy?' I ask.

'He sleeps,' she says. And then, still looking only at me, her voice as hard as flint, 'he has no right to be here.'

The painter steps forward. 'I am not a voyeur,' he says, his voice polite but firm.

I raise a hand to quiet him, see the shadow of a frown cross his face. 'He is carrying out a commission for my master,' I say slowly. 'A portrait. Of her.'

My mother silently considers this. 'It is not right,' she says finally, and I can see from the set of her jaw that there is nothing I can say to change her mind. At that moment I am poised between the three of them:

170

my mother, the dead woman, and the painter, and struggle not to lose myself within their triangle.

'It is time we left,' I say, beckoning towards the painter. I cross the room and slip out of the door, past my mother's motionless anger.

Outside, I walk briskly towards the kitchen door. 'Wait here,' I tell the painter, and I go inside to give Mary the keys. She gives me an admonishing look.

'I'm sorry,' I say.

''Twas devilish luck,' she replies.

I smile and go back out. The painter waits for me, but I cannot read his expression. We cross the ale-house yard in silence, and when we reach the road he looks at me.

'I do not understand her anger,' he says stiffly. 'A portrait is harmless enough.'

I stop short and turn to him, consider my reply. It is not easy to explain my mother's actions, and yet I would not have expected anything but her response, for I know her mind as well as my own.

'It is the *idea* of it which offends her,' I say finally. 'The great-bellied woman belonged to no one in life. To no man. My mother thinks it is wrong for him to try to own her now.'

'He wishes only to preserve her memory,' he says.

'He wishes to have her to himself, as he could not have done in life,' I reply swiftly. We stand facing each other in the darkness, and we are miles apart.

'I see,' he says finally. He frowns and turns away. It is evident that he does not see. I watch him for a

171

moment in the cold light of the moon.

'It is not just that which angers her,' I say after a moment. He looks at me expectantly, and I take a deep breath before adding, 'It is the fact of my presence there . . . with you.' I choose my words carefully, and cannot meet his eyes when I utter them. We both stare at the frozen ground, and the silence stretches out between us. And then finally his voice floats up out of the darkness.

'I apologise if I have compromised you in any way,' he says stiffly. 'It was not my intent. I only seek to carry out my commission successfully.' He clears his throat and looks away again, and I feel my heart race with anger. Perhaps my mother is right: men only seek to further their vocation. The painter and I are not partners as I had thought; I merely serve to buttress his ambitions.

I turn and walk away into the night, leaving him behind me in the cold.

Chapter Thirteen

When I was seventeen I very nearly lost myself. The man in question was called Joseph and he was an itinerant quacksalver who plied his trade throughout the county. He was some years older than I, past his thirties, though of robust good looks and youthful vigour. I first saw him at a market fair, hawking his potions with a fervency which I had rarely seen outside the pulpit. But unlike most of his kind, he seemed to me no charlatan. His belief in the healing properties of his tonic was absolute, or appeared to be so at the time. And I am ashamed to admit that my belief in him was very nearly the same.

He had no carthorse, as is common among those of his trade, but carried his stock upon his back, in a rough woven pack which lay at his feet while he spoke to the gathering crowd. But his clothes were finely cut and his hair artfully tied at the nape of his neck, and his eyes were of a brilliant blue, like the plumage of some rare bird. I stood for several minutes at the back of the crowd and listened to him expound upon the merits of his tonic – rheumatism, palsy, gout, the stone, it seemed there were no ills it could not cure. And while I was tempted to acquire some on behalf of my mother, I had not the necessary money in my pocket, so I kept my place and watched as he disposed of several bottles among the crowd. At length their numbers dwindled and only I remained, and he turned to me expectantly. He held out a bottle and I blushed and shook my head, and he stopped in front of me and pushed up his three-cornered hat so it rested precariously on the back of his head. He glanced around, saw that we were alone, and spoke with some degree of candour.

'Are you beyond the reach of ill health, or merely sceptical of nature?' He tilted his head and awaited my response, a glimmer of a smile upon his lips.

'I am neither, sir,' I replied, blushing.

'Then perhaps you are here for your amusement.'

'I thought at first to make a purchase,' I stammered. 'But find my purse is light.'

He nodded knowingly and smiled. 'A light purse is a most regrettable affliction, but it is not beyond cure,' he said. Then it was my turn to smile, for I could see he did not think ill of me.

'How much do you have?' he asked outright.

'I have but one and sixpence.'

'Then that is the price you shall pay,' he said, handing me the bottle.

'No, sir, I could not. It is too generous,' I protested.

'It is nothing of the sort,' he replied. 'The day is

long and my pack is heavy and one and sixpence will buy me a hearty supper.' And with that he pressed the murky green bottle into my hands and turned away. I watched as he disappeared into the crowds, his pack slung over one shoulder, and I was left clutching the bottle to my breast.

That night when I presented my mother with the bottle, she asked me warily from where it came, and for what price. When I told her she frowned and shook her head. 'You've paid dear,' she said. With some eagerness I explained that I had in fact received a better bargain than the others. She looked at me and sighed.

'Men who offer much for little are not worthy of your trust,' she said.

'He wanted nothing but my custom,' I said defiantly.

She raised an eyebrow. 'Such generosity does not come without its price,' she said, turning away.

'You will not even try it?' I asked, incredulous.

She turned back to me with a pointed look. 'You should not have parted with your money.'

I stared at her, too angry to speak, then snatched up the bottle and left.

Two nights later when I went out to the yard of the Great House to draw water, I heard a commotion in the chicken coop. I rounded the corner just in time to see a figure disappear inside the stable. I stood in the open doorway, struggling to catch a glimpse within the darkness. After a moment I heard a squawk and the beating of wings, and the same quacksalver emerged from the shadows, clutching a pullet by its feet.

'I thought to make a purchase, but find my purse is light,' he said.

I stared at him in disbelief before replying. 'A light purse is a regrettable affliction,' I said finally. 'How much do you have?'

He held his free hand up in the air. 'Naught,' he said. Just then the pullet squawked again. I stepped forward and held out my hand for the pullet, and he surrendered it with a grin.

'What happened to your earnings from the fair?' I asked.

'I met with ill fortune,' he said.

A gambler, I thought. I should have known. 'Another sorry affliction,' I replied.

He smiled and threw up his hands in defeat. And then he waited, and I realised that the next word would have to be mine, for I had caught him red-handed, and thievery of livestock was a punishable offence. We stared at each other for several moments. And then I spoke with as much seriousness as I could muster at the age of seventeen. 'Wait here and I will bring you a plate of food.'

When I returned he was lounging on a stack of hay, looking for all the world as if it was his rightful place. I shook my head in wonder as I handed him the wooden platter, piled high with scraps of meat, half a loaf of bread, some pickled onions and a boiled egg — whatever I could procure from the kitchen without drawing attention.

'You are too generous,' he said with the slightest trace of mockery.

I watched him eat in silence for a minute.

'The potion you sold,' I blurted out finally. 'What did it consist of?'

He stopped chewing and wiped the grease from his mouth with his sleeve. 'Naught that would do harm,' he said slowly.

'And naught that would do benefit,' I replied evenly.

He considered this. 'Optimism is a powerful tonic,' he said at last. 'And there are many who are sadly lacking in it.'

At this I could not help but smile, for I had no doubt that he was right. I stayed until he finished, and when he handed me the empty platter he tipped his hat and bowed.

'You'd best be gone,' I said.

'When you wake, you'll not remember I was here,' he said with an enigmatic smile. And then I watched as he walked out of the yard and disappeared in the dusk.

But he was wrong, for when I rose the next morning I was tinged with regret at his departure, for the world seemed to shimmer in his presence. I went about with a melancholy air that day, so much so that my mistress deemed me pale and sickly, and ordered me to retire early. But I was far too restless to do so and walked out into the spring evening, choosing a route that ended up at the stable. When I paused to look inside, I was stunned to find him there, asleep upon the same stack of hay in the corner. I approached him slowly, and as I did he woke and smiled at me.

'I came to repay my debt,' he said. And then he reached inside his purse and withdrew one and six-pence and held them out to me. I stared at the coins in his palm.

'Where did you get this?' I said doubtfully.

'An honest day's wages,' he replied.

I frowned, for work was scarce at the moment because the rains had delayed planting.

'Do not take me for a fool,' I said darkly.

'And do not take me for a common thief,' he replied, holding out his palm. 'I did not say what kind of labour,' he added.

I hesitated, then took the money. 'I suppose you require a plate of food.'

'I require nothing,' he said. 'But neither would I refuse.'

Once again I stole into the kitchen on his behalf, choosing carefully so as not to raise Cook's suspicions. This time I brought a tankard of ale as well, and when he saw it he raised an eyebrow and I blushed at the suggestion that I was favouring him. He pulled up a milking stool for me to sit upon, and chattered happily while he ate, regaling me with stories of his travels. At seventeen, I was spellbound, for apart from my mistress and the great-bellied woman, I had never met anyone who had journeyed further than London.

When he finished the ale I slipped into the Great House to replenish it, for I was as thirsty for his words as he was for the drink. When he'd emptied the second tankard he seemed to sense my dismay, and as he handed it to me he leaned forward and startled me with a sudden kiss upon the lips.

'Forgive me,' he said quietly, but did not withdraw, and when he met with my own stunned silence, he kissed me again, this time more slowly, and I remember the taste of ale upon his lips, and their unthinkable softness. This time he left me breathless, for such feelings were entirely new to me. He seemed to sense this and drew back momentarily, eyeing me.

'You've not been with a man before,' he said, and I shook my head slowly. Then he took the tankard from my hand and placed it gingerly upon the floor, and spread his cloak upon the straw while I watched, mesmerised by his movements. He turned back to me and held out his hand, and when I placed mine in it, he gently pulled me down onto the makeshift bed.

And there I lost myself to him, and to my own desires, plunging deep into the darkness of his flesh.

Afterwards I was drenched with doubt. I passed a sleepless night in my room, and rose the next morning in a turmoil. Until that day, lust had not been a part of my vocabulary. I had not been raised to acknowledge, let alone anticipate, pleasures of the flesh. The spectre of my mother was also freshly planted in my brain, uttering truths about the price of generosity. That she had been right irritated me enormously; that I had not been more resistant to his advances filled me with self-loathing. Desire and shame fought within me like sparring siblings.

At the end of our evening together he had managed to extract a promise from me to return upon the morrow, so the following dusk I prepared myself to meet him and disavow any further interest. I waited in my room until the time was right, choosing a frock that was severe and sombre in its aspect, and rehearsed my little speech of forbearance ten times over, determined not to give in once again to temptation. Finally, when I could stand it no longer, I crossed the stable yard, expecting to find him in a state of high anticipation. But all I found upon entering the stables was an empty pile of straw, whose disarray was the only clue to the previous night's occurrence. I planted myself upon the milking stool and waited three full hours for him, until the well of anger and humiliation within me rose so high I thought that I might burst. Just past midnight I crept across the stable yard and into the Great House kitchen, hoping to God that I would meet no one on the stairs.

The following morning, after a night of dreams in which he repeatedly appeared to me in the guise of various demons, I threw the green bottle and its murky tonic of optimism into the stream behind the Great House, wishing for all the world that I had never come across its maker.

For some time after, I took to reading Scripture in the evenings, hoping to purge myself of any residue of sin. After some months I managed to banish entirely the memory of that unthinkable softness, and the molten desire which accompanied it. Not surprisingly, relations with my mother improved greatly during this period, as if by renouncing any claim on the world of men I had renewed the bond between us – that cord of loyalty which binds mothers and their offspring not just at birth but, in my case at least, forever after.

Since then I have not known desire. And as I trudge along the cold, dark road, it is the knowing grin of the quacksalver which appears before my eyes. Perhaps he is my guardian angel, here to remind me of my previous sins, and steer me towards a pious future. Or perhaps he is the devil, here to taunt me with my past and lead me into despair. But he is irritating in his maleness, so I shake the image from my mind, and concentrate upon the frozen rutted road beneath my feet. It seems to me that I have once again fallen prey to circumstance. The painter clearly seized upon an opportune moment; had the taper remained lit we would not have succumbed to temptation and I would not be walking home alone in the darkest hour of the night.

But I would still have to face the wrath of my mother, who would have disapproved regardless of whether or not she had surprised us in a clench of desire. For as I told the painter, the fact of our presence there together was sufficiently damning in her eyes. My mother and her mask of betrayal would have to be reckoned with tomorrow.

When I reach the Great House I collapse into my bed, the weight of the night's events heavy upon me. I toss and turn for several hours, and when sleep finally arrives, it is troubled. In the early hours of the dawn I dream that I am caught in the vortex of a whirlpool. At the point when I am nearly lost, my mother's face appears directly overhead, looking down into the swirling water. I shout at her to help me, but my words are swallowed by the torrent and she does not hear. She peers more closely, as if she is idly curious, then turns away, disappearing from view. And then I feel myself succumb, as I am dragged down far below the surface.

Chapter Fourteen

In the morning I go directly to my mistress. To my relief, I find her awake and somewhat improved from the previous day, though she remains only the shadow of her former self. When I enter, she is sitting up in bed, propped against her cushions, staring towards the window. Cook has evidently brought her breakfast, for she clutches a small tankard tightly in her hands. She startles when she hears me, spilling some of the ale upon the bedclothes, but does not appear to notice. She turns her eyes full upon me, and I see that they are glazed with illness, like boiled sweets.

'It is you,' she says slowly. 'How long you've been away.' Her voice is heavy with the burden of infirmity.

'I'm sorry, mum. I shall not leave you today,' I reply, taking a seat beside the bed. I have already resolved to forgo any more sessions with the painter; he cannot possibly need me further, now that he has seen his subject in the flesh.

My mistress waves a hand as if to say it is no matter. She takes a sip of ale and her hand trembles as she lifts the cup to her withered lips.

'Edward remains with the painter today,' she says after a moment.

'Yes, mum,' I murmur.

'I cannot think why I wished my own portrait to be done,' she says. 'I feel that if he paints me in my present state he will rob what little life is left.' She smiles wanly at me.

'No, mum. I'm sure that is not so,' I say, but believe that she is right. At any rate, there is no question of her sitting for him; she is far too weak.

'They found her body, did they not?' she says suddenly.

I hesitate. 'Yes, mum.'

'I overheard the others,' she says. I wonder what else she has heard.

'She will be buried again soon,' I say cautiously.

'A body must be laid to rest,' she says, her eyes wide. Does she speak of herself? She turns to me. 'Edward was fond of her, you know,' she says abruptly.

I stare at her a moment before replying. 'No, mum, I did not know,' I lie.

She sighs, looks down at the half-empty cup in her lap as if she does not recognise it. 'He did not wish it to be known. But a mother has her ways.'

'There were many who admired her,' I say, somewhat at a loss for words.

'I thought perhaps that he might take a wife . . . now that she is gone.' She turns her watery gaze to me.

'Yes, mum. It is possible.' Such a thing could not be more unlikely, I think.

'I should like to see him settled before I die,' she continues. 'It is true that he has lost his youth. But he is generous of spirit, and kind of heart. His disfigurement has made him so.' She looks at me for concurrence.

'Yes, mum. He has been a good master to us all.'

'He would make an even better husband. Loyal. And true.'

Suddenly her meaning becomes clear, for it is me she has in mind. The idea fills me with both horror and astonishment. 'Yes, mum. I'm sure he would,' I stammer.

She sighs and looks away towards the window. 'He has never known the love of a woman. It would be a great tragedy if he never did.'

I think of his unbridled passion, his obsessive longing for the great-bellied woman. My mistress does not know her son is capable of such ardour, nor that he has struggled like a web-caught insect in its grasp.

'Of course there is no question of children,' she continues in a rambling tone. 'One would not want the risk. And like his father, he would not be equal to the stress. But there are other things to occupy a woman's time. A household to run. A husband to serve. These things are ample enough reward.'

'Yes, mum,' I murmur, for her mind strays now, and she does not appear to hear me.

'She would have a title. And wealth. And would bring honour to her family.' She turns back to me pointedly. In a flash I think of my mother and the closed circle of her world. My mother dwells outside the realm of wealth and titles, has no need for them, and even less desire.

'Shall I read to you, mum?' I say.

'No,' she says quietly.

'You must rest now, then,' I tell her.

'Yes.'

I take the cup from her, and as I turn away she reaches out a bony hand to grasp my arm. Her grip is surprisingly strong, and I feel a little rush of panic as she pulls me back to face her.

'You will see to it when I am gone?' she asks, her tone desperate.

I look deeply into the well of her eyes; they are awash with delirium.

'Yes, mum,' I say.

She lies back against the cushion, but does not let go of my arm, as if her hand is somehow disconnected from the rest of her. Then, almost as an afterthought, she relaxes her grip and closes her eyes, and I take up the tray and hurry from the room.

When I arrive in the kitchen, Cook shakes her head at the tray. 'She is not long,' she says with characteristic brevity.

'She may yet recover,' I reply, for I can still feel the claw of her iron grip upon my forearm.

'Death is with her now,' says Cook. 'He is there, in that room.' It is true, for I had felt it the minute I entered – a sense of decay and imminent doom. Cook shakes her head again and I see that she has assembled a bunch of medicinal herbs on the table. But they are not the usual sort, the ones that cure; they are herbs used to relieve pain and suffering, to ease one's passage into death.

'Perhaps we should send for Lucius,' I say tentatively.

Cook shrugs and lifts a cauldron of water onto the hook over the fire. 'Do what you will,' she says. 'He can do nothing for her now.'

I go at once to see my master, to inform him of his mother's condition. I find him in a state of total disarray. There is a wildness in his eyes, as if he has not slept for days. His clothes are crumpled and his face is unshaven, and his desk is a mass of open books and scattered papers. When I tell him that his mother's condition has worsened, he looks at me as if I am speaking in tongues.

'I think it best we send for her physician,' I say emphatically, hoping to impress upon him the urgency of the situation.

He nods then, finally. 'Yes of course,' he murmurs. 'I shall send a steward for him at once.' But he remains motionless, his hands frozen to the desk, and I wonder if he, too, believes her death is imminent, unstoppable. Or is it that he is half crazed with grief and longing? Truly he acts as if possessed. Perhaps Dora is more real to him in death, for now she inhabits his private world, the universe of his dreams.

'You took him to see her?' he asks suddenly.

'Yes,' I say.

He nods. 'Then surely he will be capable of rendering a likeness.'

I hesitate slightly. 'I presume so, yes.' I do not speak of her rigid death face, of how unlike it was.

'They will bury her today?'

'I have not heard, sir.'

'I should like to know,' he says.

'Perhaps I could enquire,' I suggest.

'I would be most indebted,' he replies.

I nod and turn to go, as anxious to be rid of his presence as I had been earlier of his mother's.

'There is one more thing,' he says absently. 'The painter is above. He wishes to see you, at your convenience.'

I stare at him a moment. 'I'll go at once,' I say.

I climb the stairs with mounting resentment. What more could he want from me? I pause outside his door to gather my wits. Despite my earlier resolution, it seems it will be difficult to avoid him. When I knock I hear a rustling from within, and after a moment the door opens. Like my master he is unshaven and his hair uncombed. He runs a hand through it self-consciously.

'Forgive my appearance,' he says. 'I worked late into the night.' He stands aside for me to enter. I take a step into the room, but only one, then turn to face him.

'You wished to see me?' My voice is distant, formal.

He nods. 'I worked late into the night, but she

eludes me.' He indicates the portrait on the easel, does not meet my eyes.

I cross over to look at it, and he is right. He is further from her now than before. I offer no words of encouragement.

'I cannot succeed without your help,' he says. 'I need your eyes. And your words.'

I look again upon the portrait. There is something grotesque about it, as if it, too, has died.

'I do not know,' I say hesitantly. For truly I am not sure that I can take him any further. Perhaps she is like the bird upon the mountain. Perhaps it is not possible to capture her within the frame.

'I beg of you,' he says.

I look again at him and he is on the brink of despair. Why does it mean so much to him? Is it merely a matter of pride? Or has she taken root in him as well?

'I will try,' I say finally.

He smiles a little, is visibly relieved. There is an awkward silence.

'You had better get some rest,' I say coldly. 'I'll come to you this evening.'

He nods. And then without his thanks, I go.

I send for Lucius myself, knowing that my master is incapable of making decisions, and feeling that I must do something for my mistress. When Lucius arrives, he is somewhat taken aback, for it is clear that she is fast declining. He asks to confer with her other physician Carrington, as if the burden of her care is suddenly too onerous for him alone, and so a servant is dispatched at once.

I offer him a drink and he accepts readily, suggesting we take it in the parlour downstairs so as not to disturb her, but truly it is plain that he is anxious to be free of her death-room. Her condition unnerves him and he is overly talkative, telling me he has just come from the village.

'I was asked by the magistrate to examine the body,' he explains, sipping from his glass.

'He has already arrived?' I say.

'Early this morning. Most anxious to attend the case.'

'You saw her?' I ask cautiously. Lucius nods. 'What did you find?'

'The magistrate wished to know the extent of damage. I told him it appeared their only aim was the removal of the foetus. There were no other acts of malice that I could detect. The job was crudely done but effective,' he adds, not meeting my eyes.

'Is there a suspect?' I ask.

'No. But there is talk of another search. If they find the foetus, they'll have the culprit.'

I do not reply, but it seems unlikely they will find the foetus when they could not even find the corpse.

'There is talk of sorcery,' he continues. 'Or some other of the black arts. Given the nature of the crime, I should not be surprised.'

'When is the burial?' I say, thinking of my master.

'That I do not know,' he says. 'Not immediately. The

body is the only evidence at present.'

I think of her lying there upon the sledge, of what she was, and what she has become.

Not long after, Carrington arrives. He remains frail but of a piece, and the two men withdraw to my mistress's antechamber to examine her and confer. In the meantime I send for my master, thinking he should hear their diagnosis first-hand, knowing it will reflect badly upon him if he doesn't.

He arrives looking slightly more composed, for he has shaved and combed his hair, and his shirt is clean and pressed. When the physicians emerge they return to the parlour to confer with my master, and I make a point of serving drinks again so as to be present. When I enter, there is much talk of humours and imbalance, but it amounts to little in my eyes, and they conclude by saying they wish to observe her over the next few days, rather than take immediate action. My master listens in his somewhat absent way, nodding and thanking them profusely for their efforts. As I leave, it strikes me that they are powerless, and wonder whether they themselves are aware of this.

And then I return to the kitchen, where Cook is busy brewing herbs. The smell is pungent, musky and faintly exotic, and it stirs something deep within me. For we are all secretly enthralled by death.

When I was very young, the graveyard was my haven. I went there often to play among the headstones, and over time I came to know each one: its size and shape

191

and markings. My mother told me that graveyards were the home of lost souls – those whose spirits were doomed to walk the earth forever in search of peace. This notion caught my fancy, and I resolved to search for lost souls each time I visited the place.

When I asked her what they looked like, she told me only that they could not be seen by ordinary eyes. I assumed that if I wanted to succeed, I would have to alter my vision in some way. Squinting was the most obvious means, so I would crouch behind the grave-stones for what seemed like hours with my eyes narrowed to barely more than slits. When the lost souls did not appear, I tried to tilt my head as far as possible to one side, so that the graveyard and its headstones were turned upside down.

It was in this way, with my forehead resting lightly on the grass, that I was startled one day by the bedraggled figure of a man, his face bloodied and his tunic soaked with dark stains. He came limping into the graveyard, one arm crooked tightly against his side, and collapsed not two lengths from where I hid behind a tree. He fell to his knees panting, his good arm propped in front of him, his eyes wide with pain. He stayed that way for several seconds, gasping for breath and staring at the ground, and I watched as the blood trickled from a deep wound upon his forehead, gathered on his brow, then fell in a tiny crimson thread upon the grass. He did not see me and I was terrified to move, so I watched him from my upside-down position. Here at last was a lost soul, though he was not at all what I'd expected.

After a minute he suddenly spewed up blood and with a strange gurgling sound he collapsed face down upon the earth. This was too much for me and I gave a little scream and jumped to my feet. But in the next instant I was struck by the complete stillness of his body: death had taken him as I watched. I remained motionless for several moments, and then I crept up to his side and settled myself next to him, hoping that perhaps his soul would rise up in front of me so I could follow it. I sat and watched as two big horseflies landed on his tunic, and slowly made their way across the carpet of blood. And then I was startled by sounds of shouting in the distance. After a moment a man came running towards me, followed closely by two others. The first man was also bleeding in the face, though not as badly, and when he reached me he stopped short and stared down at the body, nudging it slightly with the toe of his boot. When he was satisfied that the man was dead, he turned to his companions, who arrived huffing and puffing. All three wore the ragged clothes of vagabonds and their faces were rough and reddened from the sun.

'It's done then, is it?' said the second man, who was short and barrel-chested.

'Good as near,' said the first, wiping the blood from his face with his sleeve.

'He went easy like,' said the third with a snort of disgust. This man then placed the heel of his boot against the dead man's side and with one swift push flipped him over like a pancake. I had never seen a corpse at such close quarters, and the sight of his rolled-back eyes made me gasp. For the first time the three men looked at me, and we stared at each other for a long moment, until one of them, the one whose face was bleeding, spoke to me.

'Fell off his mount,' he said, indicating the dead man. The others nodded slowly, and then the barrel-chested man knelt down by the body. He took a knife out from under his tunic and cut loose the dead man's purse. It held almost nothing, even at my age I could tell this, and when the fat man held it up to his companions they spat and shook their heads. Then they turned and scampered off, leaving me alone with my lost soul.

When I returned home I found my mother spinning wool in front of the cottage.

'I've seen one,' I said excitedly. 'In the graveyard.'

Her eyes narrowed. 'You've seen what?' she asked warily.

'A lost soul,' I said. 'He was dead,' I added.

She looked at me a long moment, then shook her head. 'You've seen naught,' she said with a sigh, before returning to her spinning. I watched her work for a moment, knew that the force of her truth would outweigh mine, and turned on my heels and left.

Some time later I returned to the graveyard. By then the body had been removed, though I could still see the smear of blood upon the grass. My mother must have learned of the dead man in the days that followed, for news of a killing would have spread hastily about the village. But she never came to me with it, never offered her knowledge in exchange for my own.

Later that day my mistress falls into a deep sleep, and I take the opportunity to go into the village. At some point I must face my mother, but first I journey to the alehouse to discover what has happened. I enter through the kitchen door, hoping to find Mary alone, but instead find her and Samuell by the fire, their heads bowed closely in conference. They turn to me, and I see at once in their startled faces that something is amiss. Samuell nods to me and hurries from the room.

'What is it?' I ask. Mary takes a deep breath and lets it out slowly. Her face is a map of concern. 'Where is the magistrate?'

She puts a finger to her lips, and nods towards the other room. 'Within,' she says. 'Interviewing half the village.'

'And?'

'He believes there is a witch among us,' she continues, 'and has asked for a list of suspects.' She pauses then, looks into the fire. 'Your mother's name was mentioned more than once,' she says finally.

I stare at her uncomprehendingly, and think of my mother's abiding loyalty to Dora.

'It is ridiculous,' I say. 'She was her closest friend.'

Mary nods. 'I told him so,' she says.

'He interviewed you?'

She shrugs and nods.

'And Samuell?'

'Him as well,' she says.

I think for a moment. 'Who else is on the list?'

'The Widow Locke,' she says. 'And old Jack Fry.'

At this I laugh in disbelief. The Widow Locke is mad with age, and old Jack Fry a drunkard. Neither are in possession of their senses, let alone capable of such misdeeds.

'Why my mother?' I ask.

'I do not know. There is talk of a familiar.'

I cannot believe my ears, for the familiar that she speaks of could be none other than my mother's beastly cat.

'That cat has been with her less than two months,' I say angrily. 'And I know for certain she regrets the day it ever crossed her path!'

'They do not know this,' says Mary quietly.

'She has even tried to bar it from the house, but each time it howls so loudly she is forced to let it in.'

Mary purses her lips but says nothing.

I stare into the fire, see the grey cat leap within its flames, taunting me.

'Truly he is a demon of an animal,' I continue. 'And holds my mother somewhat hostage to his whims. But he is no familiar, and my mother is no witch!'

'It is not *me* you must convince,' Mary says placatingly. She lays a hand on my arm.

'What motive could she possibly have?' I say, thinking aloud.

Mary shakes her head. 'None. But there were very few who knew of Dora's condition. And your mother was one of them.' She looks at me and I know that she is right. 'And she would know how to accomplish such a thing,' adds Mary.

'She is no surgeon!' I say sharply.

'I am only repeating what others have said,' she says emphatically.

'Besides, she is growing older by the day,' I continue. 'And her health is poor. She would not be capable of moving the body.'

Mary looks at me for a long moment, and her face is grimly set.

'Not without the devil's help,' she says finally.

I see at once how quickly fate can alter the course of events. Mary is right: in the absence of any real evidence, my mother is as likely a suspect as anyone. It does not help that she is close-lipped and keeps to herself. Her silence will only serve to fuel speculation. As I make my way towards Dora's cottage, I curse the cat for ever falling in her path. That he should be the principal source of her undoing seems ludicrous.

When I enter the cottage, I find her bent over the boy, applying a poultice to his forehead. She straightens and I see immediately that though he sleeps, his face is once again flushed with fever.

'He is worse,' I say.

She nods. 'It happened in the night,' she says. 'After I returned.' She purses her lips and turns back to him.

Her reference to last night's events hovers between us like a cloud of flies.

'I am sorry for last night,' I say finally. 'It was not meant for anyone to know.'

'What you do with others is your own affair,' she says curtly. 'But the dead are sacred. And should be treated thus.' She squeezes out the poultice in a wooden bowl. The smell of dried goldenrod rises and wafts across the room. Watching her, I do not know which angers her more: seeing me embrace the painter, or allowing him to look upon Dora's corpse.

'I did not think it would do any harm,' I say, referring to the latter. 'I did not think that *she* would object,' I add.

My mother turns to me with a look of incredulity. 'How could you know this?' she demands.

There is little point to this discussion. When I meet her anger I am catapulted back in time. I stand before her, five years old, and the sins of my childhood lie heaped in front of me, so large a pile that I am dwarfed by my own misdemeanours. She makes me feel this now; that last night's misdeeds tower over me to such an extent that I could spend a lifetime in penance and still fail to atone for them. I watch her move about the room in solitary determination. As a child I thought that her anger was due to the very fact of my existence, that somehow she never forgave my bastard birth. But now it occurs to me that my worst sin is not that I was born, but that I do not share her celibate soul.

She rises again from the boy, leaving the poultice upon his forehead, and moves to the table where she takes up a knife and begins chopping herbs. Suddenly I remember the business of the magistrate. 'There is something else,' I say. She stops and looks at me. 'The magistrate has arrived and is conducting interviews. He believes there is some sorcery involved.' Her face remains impassive, and I continue, 'He has compiled a list of suspects, and your name is on it.'

She blinks, then lowers her head and resumes chopping. 'They will think what they will,' she says grimly.

'You cannot ignore them,' I say. She continues chopping, disregards me just as she will them. I move closer to the table, reach out to halt her hand.

'It is dangerous to do so,' I say emphatically.

'Neither can I stop them,' she replies.

Chapter Fifteen

Twilight falls as I return, and the atmosphere in the Great House seems taut with apprehension. I enter my mistress's bedchamber and she is lying in the stillness with her eyes wide open. She swivels her head round towards me.

'Who is it?' she asks, her voice laced with fear.

'It is only me,' I reply gently.

'You are shadow,' she murmurs. 'Nothing more than shadow.'

'Is this better?' I ask, moving closer to her side.

'It is so dark,' she says after a moment.

'Let me light a lamp.' I move to do so.

'No,' she says quickly.

I stop and turn to her. 'You prefer to be in darkness?'

She stares into the dusk. 'It is not for me to decide,' she says.

'Shall I bring your supper?'

She shakes her head slowly.

'But you must eat,' I urge. She turns to me with an

inquiring look. 'To keep your strength,' I say.

'I have no need for strength.'

'At least let me bring some broth.'

'Do what you will,' she says finally, echoing Cook's words.

Later that evening, the painter has slept and looks renewed. He paces back and forth in front of me in a state of almost feverish intensity. 'Tell me more of her,' he says, his eyes alight.

I stare at him, still irritated. 'Why?' I say.

'It will help me to see,' he replies.

'What is it you wish to hear?'

'Stories. Of her. I need to know more.' He leans forward urgently.

I say nothing; can think of nothing I wish to say. He waits patiently for me to begin, but I do not.

'Whom did she favour?' he says finally.

'She favoured no one,' I reply.

'Herself?' he asks.

'No.'

'Her son then,' he says.

'She loved him as a mother does.'

'The men who came to see her?' He presses me further. Is this what he really wishes to know?

'No,' I say definitely. But I am moving in the dark, for there is no way I can be certain of this. Was she capable of passion, of ardour, of obsessive love? I do not think so. Somehow she seemed removed from these things. Romantic love implies a degree of dependence which, to my mind, was truly foreign to her. But perhaps I did not know her.

He looks at me, weighing up my answer, judging its accuracy – or possibly my honesty.

'Was she beautiful?' he asks after a moment.

'She was striking.'

'In what way?'

I think for a moment. 'She was luminous,' I say. 'Like . . . fire seen through water.'

'Was there fire in her?'

'There was strength. And confidence. It drew them to her. She was like the bough of some great tree; something they could cling to.'

'Did you?' he asks.

'I admired her.'

'And you were drawn to her,' he says.

'Yes.'

'Like the others.'

I shake my head in irritation. 'No.'

'How then? How were you different?'

I stare at him. Perhaps I wasn't. 'We've discussed this before,' I say.

'I need to hear it again,' he replies.

'Why?'

He pauses then, looks at me as if I am forcing the words from him. 'To cleanse the image from my mind,' he says finally. He speaks of her death face, though he does not wish to say it. It haunts him.

'She is dead,' I say flatly.

'Why are you so angry?' he asks quietly.

'Because none of you will let her go,' I reply sharply. And all at once I feel exposed.

The painter turns away and crosses to the window. 'There is a story I must tell you. Perhaps I should have told it before,' he says, his tone distant and measured. As I stare at his back, his voice floats across the room. 'When I was a young apprentice, not long before my teacher died, a young woman came to stay in his household. She was some years older than I, perhaps five or six, and it was clear that she was in trouble of some kind, for she arrived in the dead of night without warning. At this time I had lived with them for five years. I had my own room in the attic of the house, and took my meals with them. The house was not very large, so when the girl arrived I moved to the studio so she could have my bed in the attic.

'My teacher would not say what trouble she was in. He told me only that she was the daughter of a friend, that both her parents were dead, and that it was his obligation to help her. She stayed with us for three weeks, awaiting passage on a ship that had been delayed by bad weather. But her presence proved a strain on the household. She was not difficult in any way; on the contrary, she went out of her way to be obliging, but my teacher became increasingly uneasy in her presence, and would leave the room on any pretext as soon as she entered. His wife, too, seemed to resent the situation, and more than once I heard them quarrel late at night after the young woman had gone to bed.

'My teacher contrived to be away a great deal during those few weeks, and I was left to my own tasks in the studio, preparing canvases and filling in the backgrounds of his portraits. The young woman often came and watched me while I worked. Because of her circumstances, she was confined to the house, and I think that she was restless and perhaps a little lonely. At first I was in awe of her. I was barely seventeen and had never known the company of women, but although she was older than me and clearly better off, I did not feel unequal in her eyes. She enjoyed watching me work, and I taught her how to mix pigments, and we talked a great deal, though she did not disclose the nature of her plight. She spoke only sparingly of her family. Like me, her parents were both dead and she had no other relations to speak of. Her mother had died the previous year of consumption, and her father had drowned in an accident some time after. She spoke a little French and German, and had inherited some means, and planned to travel to England to seek a new life.

'I was very . . . affected by her presence. I had never known anyone so bold . . . and so incapable of artfulness or deceit. Even her appearance was exceptional – perhaps especially her appearance, for although she was larger than most men, she carried herself with uncommon grace.' The painter pauses and exhales, as if suddenly relieved of a burden. He turns to face me, and as he does, his meaning becomes clear, for Dora has been with him all this time.

I shake my head in disbelief. 'You knew her.'

He nods. 'Yes.'

For a moment I am speechless.

He holds up a hand, as if to still my thoughts, and continues speaking.

'At the end of three weeks we had news that the ship she'd been expecting had foundered off the coast. By then it was apparent that she was fleeing persecution of some kind, but the arguments between my master and his wife had worsened, and it became clear that she could not remain under our roof.

'I made inquiries on her behalf but there were no other ships bound for London, so she had no recourse but to travel overland to Amsterdam, where she could be confident of securing a passage.' The painter hesitates, glancing up at me uncertainly. 'I offered to accompany her. It would have proved difficult otherwise; a young woman of her means travelling alone would have raised suspicion. Together, we could travel as man and wife, and her identity could remain a secret. We hired horses and reached the port in four days, and as luck would have it, she had only three days to wait for passage on a ship bound for England, so the matter was settled swiftly.'

He pauses then. The words 'man and wife' ring like bells within my head; try as I might I cannot quell them.

'Why did you not go with her?' I say finally.

The painter drops his head. 'Because she would not let me.'

Suddenly I see him as a boy of seventeen: vulnerable, innocent, adoring.

'What happened then?' I ask.

'She said that she would write. But if she did, her letters did not reach me. Eight years later, when I came to England, I made some inquiries, but they came to nothing. London is a big city and it is easy enough to lose oneself if one desires. But I did not realise she would seek a place as far away as this.'

'You searched for her?' I ask, incredulous. 'After *eight years?*'

'I thought perhaps to renew the acquaintance . . . that is all,' he says defensively.

I stare at him. 'You were in love with her.'

He shakes his head. 'I admired her, yes. I was . . . in awe of her . . .' He breaks off, groping for words. 'It was almost as if, when she left, some part of her stayed with me.'

'It was the other way round,' I say. 'She held you captive. Just as she did with the others.'

'No,' he says, his voice taking on a note of urgency. 'Until I met her I had not the confidence to pursue my own path. She taught me to have faith in my own vision of the world. She taught me that the hand of God is there to guide us, but that it will not spare us from peril, for in the end each of us must save ourselves.' He speaks with such intensity that the force of his words buffets me like some great wind. I grip the handles of my chair.

'Then why could she not save herself?' I say.

He pauses. 'I do not know. Perhaps she did not wish to.'

We sit in silence for a time, for we cannot move beyond this point of ignorance.

'You knew from the beginning it was her?' I ask finally.

He shakes his head. 'Something struck me that night in her cottage, when I first saw the boy. Perhaps a part of me knew then, but it was only a suspicion. Later, when I saw the body, I was certain, even though she was so very changed . . .' The painter's voice trails off.

'You should have told me,' I say accusingly.

'I never meant to deceive you,' says the painter.

I think of that night in the barn and of our chance embrace. Perhaps it was *her* he reached for in the darkness. And once this thought occurs to me, I cannot rid myself of it; it lodges somewhere deep within my gut.

'So why have you come to me again for help?' I demand. 'You knew her just as well as I.'

'I thought I did. But I realise that it is not *her* I remember, but how she made me feel.' He does not look at me when he says this, for it reveals too much of him. 'That is why I need you,' he continues, his voice barely above a whisper. 'Your words help me to remember.'

'But they are only words,' I say, my voice as hard as flint. 'They will not raise her from the dead.'

And with that I rise from my chair and push past him out of the door, nearly stumbling as I scramble down the stairs. I run along the corridors of the Great House to my room, where I collapse upon the bed. By now I am fully clad in anger; I feel it swirl around me, wash across my limbs, surround me until little else remains. I close my eyes and she is there: luminous, strong, proud, a great-bellied glory. And suddenly I wish to purge myself of her, wipe her from me like the residue of ash left from a fire.

Is it mere envy that I feel? Such a small emotion for such a deep well of feeling. I lie immobile on my bed for what seems like hours, empty my mind of all thought, concentrate on nothing. Sleep finally arrives. But as I drift into slumber, I know that she will be there in the shadows of my dreams.

Some time after, I do not know if it is minutes or hours, I wake. A noise reaches into my sleep, pulls me forth unwillingly. When I open my eyes, it is the dead of night, and I see the door to my bedchamber close slowly from without. I hear the trace of footsteps in the hall, but in an instant they are gone. Moonlight streams in through my window, casting an eerie light upon my bed. I know that I should rise and follow, but the weight of sleep is still heavy upon me. I cannot fight it, so I close my eyes and slip away.

The following morning there is no sign of disturbance in my room, nor any indication of a foreign presence, and I wonder whether the event occurred in my dreams. My mistress seems somewhat improved, though she complains at length of shadows in her eyes.

I sit with her for most of the morning, reading Scripture of her choosing. Twice she dozes off but as soon as I stop she wakes and urges me to continue. Today the task of reading is onerous. I rarely pay attention to the content – let the sounds wash over me, and find the rise and fall of my own voice comforting. But now my words sound strange and harsh. I feel as if I must spit them out into the room, where they taunt and mock me with their falsity. For today I have no certainty. My world does not conform to the one contained within these pages.

Finally she sleeps and I am free to end my recitation. The last words crackle in the silence of the room, then settle on the floor like dead leaves. I close the passage I am reading and shut my eyes. My head aches from the effort of reading and my throat is parched and rough. When I am certain she will not wake I tread silently from the room. I have heard nothing from the village and am anxious to learn news of the magistrate.

But first I go to see my mother, for the sense of duty weighs heavily upon me. When I arrive at Long Boy's cottage I am surprised to see Anne Wycombe, the ironmonger's wife, outside the door. She is bent over a washtub filled with bedclothes, and as I approach she pauses and rocks back on her heels, wiping a reddened forearm across her brow. Her hair is pulled severely back and covered by a kerchief, and the sleeves of her dark dress are rolled up to the elbows. She is a small, wiry woman of a somewhat nervous disposition who has never borne children. Some years back it was rumoured she would stop at nothing in the quest to end her barrenness, seeking out healers and soothsayers, quacksalvers and even white witches, all to no avail. There is something harsh and arid about her person, as if she herself was conceived and born of desert dryness. And age and disappointment have curdled her expression.

She catches sight of me and traces of alarm flash behind her eyes. She does not rise but nods to me nervously from her haunches.

'Good morrow, Anne. Is my mother within?' I ask.

She shakes her head and eyes me suspiciously. 'She is with the magistrate. He sent for her this morning,' she says cautiously, as if I should already have heard this news.

'Do they accuse her?' I ask.

'I know not,' she says, averting her eyes. She picks up the soap mechanically and begins to scrub the bedclothes once again.

'What of the boy?' I ask.

She stops and looks up at me. 'I am to tend him,' she says.

'Until she returns?' I ask. Anne shrugs, says nothing. Perhaps my mother is not expected to return. 'Is he still with fever?'

'It has lessened,' she replies.

I stare at her. When I was thirteen she sought counsel from my mother. She came to us in a state of great agitation, twisting her apron nervously in her fingers. My mother took one look at her and sent me out to collect firewood, for I was too old to witness her despair. I remained some time away, knowing I would meet with my mother's disapproval if I returned too soon. Finally, when my arms had grown numb from the weight of the kindling, I made my way back to the cottage. I knocked and entered and at once saw Anne Wycombe overcome with grief at the table. My mother sat immobile at her side, her lips pressed together in a thin line of concern. Expressions of sympathy do not come easily to my mother, and I saw her shift uncomfortably in her chair. When Anne saw me she stopped and raised her head, and suddenly I felt implicated in her eyes: a bastard child, an accident. She stopped crying and watched as I stacked the kindling neatly by the fireplace. And then she rose silently, her eyes flooded with the bitterness of the barren, and took her leave without another word. When the door shut behind her, my mother sighed. With one swift look she stilled my questions. We never spoke of Anne Wycombe again.

I am filled with dread as I make my way to the alehouse. I think to find Mary in the first instance, but when I enter through the kitchen it is empty, so I open the door to the main room. I recognise the magistrate at once, having seen him on one other occasion, for his looks are such that one would not easily forget the sight of him. He is seated at the table and there is no sign of my mother, nor anyone else for that matter. He is bent over a sheet of parchment, writing with the aid of an eyeglass. I enter the room silently and stand watching him for several moments, the only sound that of the repeated scratching of his quill upon the parchment. He writes slowly and precisely, pausing frequently to read what he has written. He wears a neatly powdered snow-white wig and a dark green velvet tunic fitted with a stylish white ruff, which only partly serves to conceal the folds of rosy skin beneath his chin, for he is corpulent in the extreme.

When he sees me he stops writing and lowers the eyeglass. With some effort he stands, pushing back his chair and nodding to me. I take a step forward.

'If you please, sir, it is my mother who stands accused,' I say.

He frowns, scrutinises me for a long moment, then indicates the chair opposite him at the table. 'Be seated,' he says. 'I should have sent for you this afternoon, but you have spared me the trouble.'

I take the seat opposite him, and watch as he leans back in his chair, causing the wood to creak loudly under the strain of his great weight. He pushes the papers in front of him to one side, then clears his throat and peers at me.

'The case against your mother is rather serious, I'm afraid, owing to the discovery made this morning.' He pauses then, notices my confusion.

'I assumed that you had heard,' he says, giving a little cough. 'They found the foetus buried in the clearing behind her cottage.' He watches my reaction closely, but before I can speak he holds up a hand to silence me. 'Now of course it is possible that someone else put it there deliberately to implicate her, but taken with the weight of the other evidence against her . . .' he pauses, heaves an enormous breath, as if the effort of speaking taxes him, 'in particular, the fact that few persons other than herself knew of the infant's existence, her case is very poor.'

I stare at him uncomprehending, and then I remember the bloody sack of cloth outside my mother's door. The magistrate continues, his deep voice resonating off the tavern walls. 'I am in the process of gathering statements from those who know her, and in this capacity I am, of course, most anxious to speak with yourself.'

'Sir, my mother is no witch,' I say hurriedly.

Once again he raises a hand to still me. 'Your faith in her innocence is laudable – I would wish the same from my own daughter. But I must remind you that it is a perjury and a sin to speak an untruth in this instance.'

'Sir, please listen,' I say. 'The baby they found was not the one you seek.'

'So said your mother,' he replies with a nod. 'But she refused to tell me whence it came.' He stares at me expectantly.

'It was a bastard child,' I explain. 'Born still to a young girl across the river. My mother delivered the infant. The girl in question had concealed the pregnancy from her relations, and when it was born dead, she asked my mother to remove it and give it a proper burial.'

'You were there?' he asks.

'No, sir.'

'You know the whereabouts of the young woman in question?'

'No, sir.'

'Her name then?'

I sigh, and shake my head. 'My mother did not tell me.'

He gives another enormous sigh and shifts again in his chair; for a moment I am convinced it will collapse under his bulk.

'That is more information than your mother gave us, though it is still insufficient to clear her of suspicion. Tell me this: why does she fail to speak in her own defence?'

'My mother does not break an oath lightly.'

He ponders this a moment, his fleshy face folded in a frown. 'She will have to do so if she wishes to clear her name,' he says finally.

'Sir, my mother is a God-fearing woman who has dedicated her life to helping women birth children. Surely the people of the village have told you this.'

'They have told me many things,' he says slowly.

'They have not spoken on her behalf?' I ask, incredulous.

'She appears to have few advocates,' he says.

'But surely she has even fewer enemies,' I counter.

He shrugs. 'The practice of witchcraft is common among those of her trade.'

'But she has bewitched no one,' I protest. 'A body

215

has been taken, but aside from this, what harm has befallen anyone?'

He looks at me sternly. 'May I remind you that theft from a grave and the desecration of a corpse are extremely serious offences. But aside from this, there is the matter of the boy and his condition to consider.'

I cannot believe my ears. 'My mother has tended him faithfully since his mother's death,' I say slowly.

'And he has deteriorated steadily under her care,' he replies evenly.

'You suspect her of bewitching him?'

'It is indeed likely,' he answers.

'What motive could she possibly have? She had no quarrel with the dead woman,' I say.

'None that we are aware of. But the woman in question died under extremely mysterious conditions. It appears to me that her death was not the result of an accident, as had been originally supposed.'

I am silent for several moments. 'What evidence do you have in support of this?' I ask cautiously.

'At this stage, none,' he replies. 'But my instinct tells me there is more to learn about the circumstances of her death.'

I sit opposite him, my mind whirling. I cannot tell him that I share his intuition; neither can I divulge what I know without endangering my mother.

'Did you question my mother about her death?' I ask finally.

'No. But I intend to. In the meantime there are others in the village I must interview. I have ordered your mother to remain in her cottage for the present, until we have further need of her. She is not to go near the boy. Have you anything else you wish to say on her behalf?'

I look at him, and slowly shake my head.

'Then you are free to go,' he says.

The village seems deserted as I make my way towards her cottage, as if people have locked themselves away with their suspicions. The few people that I pass avert their eyes; it seems that news has travelled quickly. I wonder that I did not hear of it earlier, then decide that perhaps my ignorance was not an accident, for people are surprisingly quick to ally themselves with gossip of any kind.

When I open the door to my mother's cottage, I find her seated at the table, motionless. Her hands rest delicately on the table in front of her, as if she is about to play an instrument, and it strikes me that I have rarely, if ever, seen them idle.

I close the door and seat myself opposite her. Though she is not yet a prisoner, already she wears the look of one. 'I've come from the magistrate,' I tell her. She looks up at me expectantly, and I realise I have nothing positive to offer her. 'The case against you is serious. Do you realise this?' I lean forward, place my hands upon the table opposite her. Another daughter might have clasped her hands in reassurance, but though I urge myself to do so, I find that I cannot. She says nothing, continues staring at the table.

'You must tell them everything,' I say. 'You must tell the truth.'

'The truth will be a weapon in their hands,' she says.

I sigh and look at her. She is remarkably calm. Or perhaps she is resigned, just as my mistress is to death.

'Tell me where to find the girl. Surely she would not object if she knew you were in danger?'

My mother slowly shakes her head.

'You pay too great a price with your silence,' I say. 'You do not owe her this.'

'She was a traveller. I do not know her where-abouts,' she says. I wonder if she tells the truth. Nonetheless, there must be some other means of proving her innocence.

'The baby you delivered. Did it come to term?' I ask.

'It was born early,' she says in a wooden voice.

'How early?'

She shrugs. 'Some weeks,' she replies.

'How many? Three? Six?' I urge her to remember.

'Perhaps six. I do not know, I never met the mother during the course of her confinement.'

The fact that the baby was not fully formed makes it harder to distinguish from the foetus taken from the great-bellied woman. My mother looks at me grimly, for she is well aware of this. I sit back in my chair, look around me at the simply furnished cottage.

'Then we must wait,' I say finally. 'And see what they decide.'

That evening I take my food alone in my room, as I have no wish to confront the likes of Rafe and Alice in the great hall. When darkness is complete, I take my cloak and leave by the front door unseen, anxious to find Mary at the alehouse.

When I enter through the rear door I am relieved to see her there, bent low over the kitchen fire. She straightens at once when she sees me, wiping her hands upon her apron.

'I've been at Chepton until this evening,' she says, her eyes filled with concern. 'I only heard the news just now.' I tell her what I know about the infant they found, and she shakes her head in dismay. She forces me to sit and ladles some broth from a pot over the fire.

'You are pale,' she says, placing a wooden bowl in front of me. 'This will do you good.' I sip the hot broth.

'Have you heard anything else?' I ask anxiously.

She nods a head towards the other room. 'It is very full within. They lose their heads when they drink – men's tongues are even looser than their wives'.'

'They speak of her?' I ask.

She rolls her eyes. 'There is no one they *do not* speak of. Every crooked woman is a witch, every stray animal harbours the devil, and every sick cow is a victim of enchantment.' She shakes her head. 'It has gone too far.' She reads the fear in my eyes and lays a reassuring hand upon my arm. 'It will come to naught,' she says.

'What if it doesn't?' I reply.

Just then the door opens and the painter stands awkwardly in the doorway. Mary straightens and he nods to her.

'Forgive me,' he says.

She motions him in, then picks up a tray and excuses herself, disappearing through the door behind him. He turns to me.

'I looked for you at the Great House,' he says. I do not offer a reply. What could he possibly want? He takes a step forward into the room. 'I heard the news about your mother,' he continues. Our eyes meet for a moment.

'She is innocent,' I say finally, looking away.

'I did not think otherwise,' he says. 'But it is strange, this accusation, is it not?' He looks at me inquiringly.

I sigh. He is an outsider, does not understand our ways, nor the damage that simple minds and idle talk can do.

'There has been much talk,' I say. 'It will likely come to nothing.' I echo Mary's words, unsure if I believe them. He is about to speak when Mary enters, carrying several empty tankards. He watches her a moment, then turns to me once more.

'I am sorry,' he says quickly, then disappears through the door.

Mary raises her eyebrows. 'For what does he apologise?' she asks.

I think of Dora and his revelation of their past. Is he

sorry for his deception? Or his devotion?

'I do not know,' I say.

She smiles grimly and shakes her head, begins to douse the tankards in a bucket.

'How goes the portrait?' she asks after a moment, wiping her hands on her apron.

'The dead do not sit still,' I say.

She looks at me and smiles.

Chapter Sixteen

The next morning my mistress appears somewhat revived; her colour has improved and the glassiness has gone from her eyes, though it is clear they are failing. She agrees to take some breakfast and I prepare a tray for her under Cook's supervision: nothing cold and nothing solid, she admonishes, only that which has been well-cooked and sieved. My mistress frowns when I set the tray in front of her, but she eats slowly and finishes most of it. At length she pushes the remainder aside.

'Edward came to see me this morning,' she says cautiously. 'He told me of your mother's predicament.' She regards me closely, and I sigh inwardly. Even on her sickbed she is not beyond gossip. 'I urged him to intervene on her behalf,' she continues. 'Though I know not what he can do.'

'They do not accuse her at present,' I say.

'No doubt they will, if no one else is found,' she replies. She looks towards the window. 'It does not bring honour upon the Great House,' she says at length.

I gaze at her. I thought her talk of marriage between Edward and me had been born of her delirium, but apparently the notion remains planted firmly within her. With horror, I wonder whether she has spoken to him of it, and hope fervently that she has not.

'I am sorry, mum,' I say.

She turns to me and nods beneficently. 'The Lord will steer us free from peril.'

I do not share her confidence.

Later, she sleeps, and I go to visit Long Boy, as I have promised my mother I will watch over him. When I arrive at the cottage Anne Wycombe admits me with a brief nod and scarcely a word, then carries on with her sewing in the corner of the room. Long Boy is sitting up in bed and is of good colour, though his eyes are strangely bright.

'Where is your mother?' he asks at once. Anne raises her head at the question, but when I glance in her direction she lowers it quickly, as if I have caught her eavesdropping.

'She is resting at home,' I tell him.

'Is she ill?' he asks, uncomprehending.

'No. She is only tired,' I say. 'But she'll soon return.'

Long Boy nods; this seems to satisfy him. Anne frowns but says nothing.

'How do you feel?' I ask him.

'I am well,' he answers matter-of-factly. Perhaps he does not recall the fever of the past few days. He nods towards Anne. 'Will this woman stay with me?' he asks.

'I do not know,' I say, for truly I do not.

'Whose mother is she?' he asks. It is an innocent enough question, but it hits the mark. Anne rises quickly, and taking up the leather strap used to carry kindling, leaves the cottage without a word.

'She has no children,' I explain when she has gone. 'That is why she has been asked to look after you.' He frowns slightly, as if this somehow cannot be. 'Have you eaten?' I ask. He does not answer, merely stares at the closed door through which Anne has just departed. 'Long Boy, are you hungry?' I say a little more loudly. At length he turns to me, his eyes dark and troubled.

'My mother is cold,' he says finally.

I think of all the things that I could say in response, but something tells me I must tread carefully, for there is turmoil in his eyes.

Instead I bring him broth and bread, and he eats hungrily, absently, just as he did before the illness. While he is eating, Anne returns, loaded with kindling, and begins to stack it in a pile by the fire.

'I want to go out,' says Long Boy, his mouth filled with bread. I glance in Anne's direction and she frowns.

'Not yet,' I answer. 'You must rest.'

'When?' he asks immediately.

I nod towards Anne. 'She will tell you when the time has come,' I say. He looks at her darkly and I read disapproval in his eyes. 'Perhaps soon,' I say pointedly, and Anne nods tentatively. 'I must go now,' I tell Long Boy.

'Where?' he asks.

Anne looks at me and our eyes lock.

'To my mother,' I reply.

The boy troubles me, for although the fever has gone, it has clearly left its imprint on him. As I approach my mother's cottage, I see a small crowd standing outside. Samuell stands in front of the door facing them, and nods to me grimly. The dozen or so people speak among themselves, but when they see me, silence falls upon them like a shroud. I cross at once to Samuell, who takes my arm and eases me away from the others.

'What happens here?' I demand.

He looks at me uneasily. 'The magistrate has ordered a search,' he says in a hushed tone. 'Goodwife Locke and Widow Frye are within.'

'They search her person?' I ask.

He nods.

'May I at least attend them?'

He shakes his head. 'None but the two, according to his orders. And they shall report their findings directly to him.'

I turn towards the crowd. Most of them do not meet my eyes.

'Why are they here?' I say angrily after a moment, raising my voice so they will hear. A few murmur in response. 'What business have you here?' I shout. Samuell lays a hand upon my arm. I turn back to him.

'Please,' he says urgently. 'I will bring the women back to the alehouse, and the crowd will no doubt follow.'

I nod slowly. A few in the crowd have shuffled silently away. The others hang their heads like stray dogs.

'How long have they been within?' I ask Samuell.

He bites his lip. 'Some time now,' he replies. I think of my mother and her fiercely private nature. She must have known that it might come to this, for a search is often done in cases where witchcraft is suspected.

After another minute, the door to the cottage opens and Goodwife Locke and Widow Frye emerge silently, their eyes masked in secrecy. The crowd stirs a little, presses forward around them, but Samuell moves swiftly forward with authority and ushers them away. The two women bow their heads discreetly and he leads them away towards the alehouse. A few in the crowd follow at a distance; the others gradually disperse.

I wait until they have all gone, then approach the cottage door. I knock gently, then open it and poke my head inside.

'Mother?' The room is dark and it takes a moment before my eyes find her in the poor light. She is perched upon the side of the bed, her hands clasped tightly in her lap, her head bowed. At the sound of my voice, she lifts her head and I let myself in, carefully bolting the door behind me. I cross over to her side and sit beside her on the bed.

'Are you all right?' I ask. She nods, just barely, but everything about her has gone rigid, as if her very centre has been frozen. Her face is white and drawn, and her lips are pressed together in a taut line. Only her eyes betray her horror.

'It is done now,' I say gently. She turns to me then, shakes her head slowly from side to side. 'What is it?' I ask.

She starts to speak, then swallows her words and closes her eyes.

'Surely they found nothing?' I ask urgently. She sighs deeply, and with her eyes still closed she places a hand gently on her side, beneath her ribs. In that spot, under her clothes, she carries a scar from long ago. 'The scar,' I say. She opens her eyes, lets her hand fall into her lap.

For all my life my mother has carried this scar. It is the length and breadth of a finger and is raised and reddened, though the colour has altered somewhat over the years. Now that she is growing old, the skin around the scar hangs down in fleshy folds, giving it a slightly protuberant look. I have never known its origin; only that it has always been a part of her. Once when I was very young, she lifted me upon her hip and as she did I reached a tiny hand to touch it. Her whole body bristled and she dropped me like a sack of flour. I lay on the floor crying, and she stood silently over me, her chest heaving with anger. I never tried to touch it again.

'What of the scar?' I ask her urgently. 'What did they say?'

She turns to me and for the first time raises her

head to meet my eyes. 'They say it is the devil's teat.'

'You told them otherwise?' I ask slowly.

'Yes, of course. I told them it was from a wound. That I have had it many years. Have carried it most of my life,' she adds. She lapses into sullen silence. I wait for her to continue.

'What did they say?' I press her.

She turns to me with a look of disbelief in her eyes. 'It makes no difference how many years, do you not see?' She shakes her head from side to side. 'They will think what they wish.'

'No. This cannot be. Did they ask you where it came from?'

She nods.

'Did you tell them?' I ask this quietly, for this is something even I have never asked of her.

'I told them it was from a man,' she says, her voice hardening. And suddenly her eyes are wide and far away, lost in time.

'What man?' I ask, though I know full well the answer.

She looks directly in my eyes. 'Your father,' she says.

And then it strikes me that they are right: my father *was* the devil and he has left his mark upon her. I turn to her and she is hunched over: the carcass of a woman.

'Who was he?' I ask.

'It makes no difference,' she says without emotion. 'He is dead.'

'How did it happen?' I persevere.

She stares ahead of her. 'It was . . . so long ago,' she says, shaking her head. 'I was someone else then. Younger than you are now.' She reaches up a hand to touch my face, but her hand halts in mid-air, then drops into her lap. 'I had not yet begun to birth babies, though I often assisted my own mother. I helped my father as well, in the fields, and with the cows. He sold his milk to many others in the village.' She pauses, lowers her voice. 'And to the Great House.'

Something in her tone makes me frown. She has always shunned the Great House. Before I went to work there, I never knew she'd entered its borders. After a moment, she carries on.

'I went there thrice weekly. With milk and butter we had churned ourselves. There was never enough to satisfy them; they always wanted more. We kept very little for ourselves. My father was anxious to build a small herd. We had three dairy cows but he wanted half a dozen. And so we scrimped and saved and did without. And then one morning early in spring I rose at dawn to do the milking and found the cows dead in the field. They must have died early in the night, because by the time I got to them, they were stone cold, and the birds had found them first. I was afraid to tell my father, for his temper could be fearsome, and my mother was away. She had left the previous evening to birth a child and had not yet returned.

'I found him in the barn sharpening his scythe, and when I told him of the cows, he dropped his tools and ran straight to the fields. I followed at a distance, and by the time I arrived his face was wrecked with bitterness. He turned and looked at me as if I was a complete stranger, and I knew then that he was lost. He left me in the fields with the carcasses, and shut himself inside the house with all the drink that he could lay his hands on. I waited for my mother to return, but she did not. In the late afternoon I finally walked up to the Great House to tell them there would be no milk. I called at the kitchen, as was my custom, but when I found it empty I made a tour of the barns, searching for a stable hand. Not a soul was about. I found out later they had all gone to the chapel for a christening. My mother had birthed the baby not two weeks earlier, to a serving girl on the estate.

'I thought I heard a noise from the stable, so I went inside. It was dark and I could see a horse in the box at the far end, a large chestnut mare. Someone was behind her but I could not make out who, so I took a step further in and called out. I must have frightened the mare for she started and backed up within the stall, and then I heard a man swear, for the horse had trod upon his foot. I could tell at once that he was drunk, just as my father was at home. And then he came round and showed his face, and I recognised the master of the Great House, your master's father.' She pauses then, looks at me briefly, then looks away, the memories crowding her.

'He was old and ugly with drink. There had been much talk of him that spring, for he'd nearly killed a serving man in his employ not three weeks earlier. He had thrashed him with a horsewhip for the tiniest offence. But the rich do not get punished for their sins, and the matter had never come to trial, though the man in question afterwards went lame and lost an eye.' She shakes her head, takes a deep breath.

'He was . . . an evil man. All those who worked at the Great House suffered as a consequence. I would not have let you near there had he remained alive. But he died a dog's death two years later, and I thanked the Lord the day I heard.' She turns to me as if the tale is told, and then I see a shadow cross her eyes.

'What happened in the stable?' I ask gently. I see her chest rise and fall, her breath coming sharply.

'He came round the horse towards me and his face was twisted with anger. I apologised for giving fright to the mare, but when I tried to leave he grabbed my arm and asked me what my business was. I told him why I'd come, and once again I tried to take my leave. But he held me firm. He asked if I could saddle a horse. When I answered yes he forced me towards the mare. I did not know what had gone before, but its eyes were white and round with fear. I did not like the look of her and said that we should take her out into the yard. He shook his head and ordered me forward. The horse was two heads taller than myself and nearly filled the stall. As soon as I went near, she began to thrash from side to side. I truly thought that I might perish if I went into that stall, and I turned and told him so.

'When I did, I saw that he was partially unclothed. He'd taken off his doublet and all that remained were his shirt and breeches. That is when I saw the knife. It was small and silver with a pearl handle, a gentleman's knife, but I could see the blade hanging by his side. He took a step towards me and I remember thinking that I had nowhere to run, for the mare was behind me and he was in front. He took another step and the mare startled. She jumped and kicked at me and I was knocked forward by her feet. She'd kicked the air from my chest and I fell upon the ground not two steps from where he stood. He waited until I sat up, then he grabbed my arm and dragged me to the stall opposite. I struggled at first and he held the knife up to my face and said that he would cut me. I could smell the stench of liquor on him, so I kept my place. But he would not be satisfied, could not do at first . . . what needed to be done. This made him even more angry, and he hit me with his fist several times about the face and body. And then he held the knife and forced me to . . . revive him . . . until he was able to finish.' My mother pauses then, her chest heaving from the effort of the memory, her eyes filled with pain. I place a hand upon her arm and she flinches without even realising. At length, she continues.

'The mare was our witness. I stared over his shoulder into her eyes and wished that I had chosen her instead. Afterwards I began to cry, and once again he grew angry. He ordered me to stop but I could not and then he drew the knife again and said that he would cut me if I could not be silent. Just then there was a noise in the yard and when I screamed he took the knife and slashed me here. The door to the stable opened for a moment. I looked but could see no one, for I was on the floor. But he could see. He screamed at the person to leave us, and then I heard the footsteps of a child run away across the yard.

'He left me then, cursing the child. There was much blood upon the floor from the wound and the smell of it all around. The mare stood watching me, and suddenly she was calm. It was then I saw the blood upon her chest, for he had cut us both. I waited there with her until darkness fell. By then the blood had stopped and I was able to walk home, where I found my father unconscious on the floor from too much drink. I dressed the wound as best I could, and waited for my mother to return.

'She came at dawn the following morning, tired and upset because the baby was born still after more than two days of labour. My father woke and was still mean with drink. There was so much desolation in the house. All that we had worked and saved for had been lost. Or so it seemed that morning.' She shakes her head and stops talking.

'Did you tell her?' I ask quietly.

She lifts her head to look at me. 'I found that I could not,' she says. 'I caught a fever and spent some days in bed. By the time I recovered, the wound was nearly healed, though the scar remained. My mother did not see it until many months later, long after I knew I was

pregnant. By then she did not want to ask. By the time
you were born, my father had run off and drunk
himself to death. My mother died of smallpox the
following spring. It was a miracle that you and I were
spared.'

I stare ahead, cannot picture the young woman in
the tale, cannot fathom that it is my mother, nor that I
myself have played a central role. But most of all, it is
the idea of my father that I cannot stomach. And the
terrible violence from which I came. Something rises
up in me: the need to purge myself of the story seeded
deep within. But my mother begins anew, and I raise
my head to listen.

'When you first went to work at the Great House, I
felt some fear. As if the house itself was partly respons-
ible for what had happened. But I told myself that he
was dead, and that your mistress seemed a decent and
charitable woman. I had seen her many times about
the village, and though we'd never met, I had a sense
that she, too, had suffered at his hands. And the child,
the boy: his tragedy was clear enough for all to see.
Somehow I thought that we were joined to them by
suffering, and though I could not bring myself to enter
the Great House, it seemed both right and natural for
you to be under its roof.' She looks at me for confirmation of this choice, or perhaps for absolution, but I
find that I am too stunned to offer it.

'Why did you not tell me earlier?' I ask at length.

'What purpose would it have served?' she says.

Perhaps she is right. Some truths are only agents of

suffering. And yet I had a right to know. For I am like the scar upon her belly: we are what remains.

We sit in silence, trussed in memory, until darkness falls. And by the end of day a curious thing occurs: our silence forms a kind of harmony. It is the first time I have felt anything like companionship with my mother.

I leave her finally and return to the Great House, for there is nowhere else to go, and it seems as if the walls themselves exert some power over me, pull me back within their confines. I have forgotten entirely about my mistress in the interim, and when I enter through the kitchen, Cook looks at me a little strangely, as if something about my person has altered.

'She asked for you,' she says, nodding upstairs. I stare at her, do not reply. 'I told her your mother was in need,' she adds.

'It was the truth,' I say without explaining further. I turn and leave the kitchen, make my way towards the great hall and its portrait gallery. It is there I find him, and he is waiting for me. The portrait seems almost alive; his eyes are full of venom and they lock me in their gaze. Perhaps my mother is wrong, perhaps I do not belong beneath his roof. But the portrait holds me frozen to the spot. I stand for several minutes until I hear a noise behind me. I tear my eyes from those up on the wall and turn to see the painter at the end of the gallery. He watches me intently, and the look upon his face is uncomprehending.

'Are you all right?' he asks, taking a step forward.

I shake my head and push past him, run up the stairs to the haven of my room, where I collapse into sleep.

But I cannot stop him from my dreams. He comes to me just as he is in the Great House portrait: a man of forty-odd years, tall, dark-complected, stern of visage. In my dream he is perched upon the giant mare, clutching a whip tightly in his hand. And then I see that she is drenched in blood. It oozes through her chestnut coat as if through a carpet, and the foam flies about her mouth. He urges her forward and she takes a step then falters, her long legs trembling. He begins to beat her savagely with the whip, and she meets my gaze for one brief moment, then collapses under his weight, the whites of her eyes glistening. He rolls free from her and with one swift movement draws the pearl-handled knife and slits her belly lengthwise like a vast ripe fruit. The skin of her belly opens and out tumbles the boy, the crooked boy, fully clothed and blinking back his fear. His father raises the whip and the boy stumbles to his feet and runs away, leaving his father shouting obscenities in his wake. I watch the boy disappear round the corner of the yard, and when I turn back to the master, his demon eyes glow red. He sees me now, raises the whip in my direction, but when I try to run I find that I am frozen to the spot. The mare's blood runs in rivers across the soil, and soon it surrounds me like the tide. I glance down at my feet and they are awash with her suffering.

Chapter Seventeen

I wake uneasily, with a strong sense that I must act quickly before my mother's fate is wrenched from our hands. The other servants are already huddled over their bread and prayers when I descend. I pause just outside the great hall and listen to the low but steady murmur of voices and the occasional peal of laughter. When I enter, silence falls over them and a row of inquiring eyes greets me. I think of the scar upon my mother's belly and wonder whether the women have maintained their silence. If so, it is only a matter of time, for the devil's teat is too powerful a secret to lie buried for long. I do not sit with them, but cross directly to the kitchen, where I find Cook already with her hands deep inside a pullet. She raises her head and her eyes flood with concern.

'How goes your mother?' she asks tentatively.

'As well as one might expect,' I reply.

She shakes her head and sucks in air through her teeth, then slowly extracts her hands from the pullet, her fists clutching entrails. In a flash I see the image from my dream: that of the crooked boy spilling forth from the riven belly of the mare. And all at once I know what I must do.

My master is an early riser, and I am not surprised to find him already seated at his desk in the library. As I enter the room it strikes me that perhaps he has remained rooted there throughout the night, for it is clear from his demeanour that sleep has barely visited him these past few days. He reminds me of Long Boy, for his eyes hold the same restless look about them. My unannounced visits no longer take him by surprise, and I do not feel trepidation in his presence, only urgency, as if the burden of my mother's story should not be borne by me alone.

I speak slowly, cautiously, choosing my words with precision. I tell the tale in its entirety, just as it was told to me, and as I do, am taken aback by the pleasure I feel to see the look upon his face. For he is truly horrified, just as I knew he would be. Indeed, his embarrassment is so acute that I can almost touch it. His crooked spine seems to contort with shame as I speak, so much so that as I near the end of the tale he is bent so far to one side that his face nearly rests upon the desk. It is as if all the sins of his father have somehow lodged themselves within his very bones. When I finish, there is a long silence during which the only sounds are that of the timepiece ticking in the corner and the rise and fall of his own laboured breath. At length he straightens, unfolding himself as best he can, and looks at me.

'I was that child,' he says quietly. He takes a deep breath before continuing. 'And the image of my father . . . drunken, half-clothed, a bloodstained knife in his hand, has never left me. I did not see the woman, your mother, though I heard her screams. They, too, have stayed with me . . . it is not the sort of thing a child easily forgets.' He pauses then, his eyes brimming with pain, then clears his throat.

'My father hated me,' he says in flattened tones. 'I suppose my . . . infirmity was too great a disappointment. Or perhaps I was simply made to pay for his mistakes. Sometimes I think my whole life has been lived entirely in atonement for his. Does that sound self-pitying?' He looks at me and I slowly shake my head.

'At any rate, when he died I felt relief . . . though little else had changed. At least I no longer had the spectre of his anger to confront.' He gives me a small half-smile. 'Only its memory.' He looks away then, lost in that other time.

I consider whether I should reveal the final chapter of my tale. My mother's voice comes to me: what purpose would it serve? But something propels me forward, like a wave sweeping across the shore.

'My mother fell pregnant,' I say. 'She never married. There were no other men . . . neither before, nor after,' I add, lest my meaning be unclear.

He stares at me, his eyes widening with realisation. 'I see,' he says finally.

'You must help us,' I continue. 'You must help *her*.'

'Yes,' he whispers. 'Yes, of course.'

'You must go at once to the magistrate. And you must tell him what you saw,' I say.

His face fills with confusion. 'But I did not see him cut her. Indeed, I did not see *her* at all. I saw only him . . . and the blood upon the knife.'

I trap his gaze firmly in my own. 'Then you must lie,' I say.

He nods slowly.

And then, in minute detail, I describe the scar and its location.

I leave him stunned, and go directly to my mistress. As I enter her bedchamber I can think of nothing other than her husband, my father. The knowledge lies deep within me, like a coiled snake. If she suffered under him, then she has cloaked it well, for nothing in her passing references has ever led me to suspect the depth of his sins. Her comments were disguised by propriety and a thinly veiled ambivalence. Perhaps she closed her eyes to his brutality. Perhaps he kept it from her – but this seems unlikely, as she is shrewd and aware. It makes her somehow tragic in my eyes. Almost more so than my mother, for though my mother was a victim, she was not complicit in her own undoing.

My mistress is asleep when I arrive, the skin on her cheeks like oiled paper. I rearrange the bedclothes and she stirs, opening her eyes. She blinks repeatedly, endeavouring to focus her gaze, but in the end she appears to fail, for she rolls over to one side with a sigh and closes them anew. I wait a few moments, until her breathing is more regular, then quietly slip away. I do not think that she has seen me: her servant, the daughter of her husband.

I hurry to my mother's cottage, and find her busy washing wool. At least her hands are occupied, a sign that her spirits have improved. She greets me with relief and appears almost grateful for my visit, though she wears her gratitude uneasily, like an ill-fitting garment.

'Have you seen the magistrate?' I ask at once.

She shakes her head. 'I have heard nothing,' she says.

'You have not been accused?'

'Not to my face.'

'Well, that is something at least,' I reply. She lifts the wool out of the basin and wrings the water from it with both hands. I watch as she squeezes out the last remaining drops.

'I have been to see my master,' I say quietly. She pauses, her hands in mid-air, and raises her head to look at me, the newly washed wool hanging limply from her fingers. 'He was the boy that day,' I say.

'I have always known as much,' she replies. Without thinking, she drops the wool once again into the water.

'He will intervene on your behalf. He will tell them what he saw that day: the truth about the scar.'

She looks down at the cloudy water in the basin, the wool floating freely like an island. Instinctively her arms move to clutch her sides in a protective embrace. I read her thoughts in an instant: it is all too public, this airing of her past. Even worse than yesterday's search, for that was between women, behind closed doors. But the idea of two strange men discussing what befell her at the hands of a third: this she cannot bear.

I lay a hand upon her shoulder. 'It must be done,' I say gently. She nods, just barely. I remove the wool once again from the water and wring it tightly in my hands. Even with my master's help we cannot guarantee her safety. The only thing that will truly change their minds is the discovery of Dora's foetus. But that remains a riddle none of us can solve.

At length my mother takes the wool from my hands and methodically hangs it out over a wooden frame by the fire.

'How is the boy?' she asks finally.

'The fever is gone,' I say hesitantly. 'But he is somehow altered.'

'She feared for him,' my mother says slowly.

'How?' I ask.

'She told me once, not long ago . . . that it was ill-judged of her to raise a child in the constant company of strangers.' My mother looks at me, her meaning evident. When he was young, Long Boy remained behind a bed curtain when his mother entertained. Later, when he was old enough, he was sent outside, though often I'd see him crouching close behind her cottage, as if he could not bear the separation. In truth, such was her calm assurance and easy manner that no one gave a second thought to the propriety of his presence. He was like an extra limb, almost a physical extension of herself. But now that she was gone, it seemed as if the life source had been wrenched from him.

'It did not help that he was so unlike the others of his age,' says my mother, referring to his size. I had never seen him play with other children; he looked a giant in their presence. Like my master, his body was a cage, isolating him from others. It stood in sharp contrast to that of his mother, for hers was like a fountain of abundance, where all and sundry could come and replenish themselves, drink deeply of her generous spirit.

'Perhaps when he reaches manhood he will be more settled,' ventures my mother. She looks at me and our eyes meet in a frown.

She does not believe this, and neither do I.

I take him bread that she has baked, and when I place it in his hands, he holds it gingerly, staring down into the deep brown crust as if it will contain her likeness. He raises his head and looks at me expectantly.

'Is she still tired?' he asks.

I nod. 'She needs to rest,' I say. 'But when she has regained her strength, she will return.'

He frowns, looks down again at the bread. 'Your friend was here,' he says. I stare at him blankly. 'He left me that,' he says, nodding towards the table.

I cross over, see the charcoal sketch upon the table for the first time. It is of the boy, seated up in bed, the same look of turmoil in his eyes. I hold the paper and my hands tremble slightly. I turn to Anne Wycombe.

'He was here?' I ask.

She hesitates, then nods. 'Yesterday,' she says.

'But . . . why?' I ask.

'To see the boy,' she answers.

'He asked to draw my picture,' says Long Boy proudly. 'It is very like, is it not?'

I cross over to his side and together we study the drawing. Long Boy reaches out and fingers it, clearly entranced by his own image.

'Yes,' I say slowly. I have hardly said two words to the painter these past few days, yet the anger has not lessened over time.

'He said he was a friend of yours,' says Long Boy.

I look at him, feel the rage rise within he. 'He has been hired by my master,' I reply.

This seems to satisfy Long Boy, for he nods, then bites off a hunk of my mother's bread. But it does not satisfy me, for I do not trust the painter's motives.

'You must be wary of such gifts,' I say, echoing my mother's words.

'It was not a gift,' says Long Boy. 'He called it an exchange.'

I look at him, puzzled, and then it dawns on me. 'You gave him the book.'

Long Boy nods and his eyes colour anxiously at the tone of my voice. 'He said he would return it. He will, won't he?'

I leave him, clutching my fury like a tightly wrapped parcel. The painter's interest in her now seems like an act of trespassing; he has no right to be here and even less claim upon her than the others, for it seems to me that the woman he knew was not the same as the one who lived within our midst. If only he would leave; take his charcoal and his sketches and his disquieting vision with him.

When I reach the Great House, I go at once to the tower, can think of nothing else but the need to retrieve the diary and tell him he must go. My heart races as I climb the stairs and by the time I reach his room, my chest is heaving with rage. I stop sharply at the door, for it stands slightly ajar, and I struggle to regain my composure; I have no desire to make a fool of myself in front of him. But all is silent within; I hear only the sound of my own breath. Instead of knocking, I raise a hand and ease the door open slightly. At once I see his room is empty, and I enter quietly, like a thief, closing the door behind me.

My first thought is that he has already left the village, and I feel a stab of disappointment until I see that this is not the case, for the room still holds his things. The bed is made up tidily and his few belongings are stowed neatly to one side, almost as if he were expecting someone. His paints and canvases are stacked upon a table in the corner of the room, together with his papers and sketches. I cross over to them, wonder what, if any, progress he has made these past few days. But what I see on top of the pile is not her face, but my own, staring out at me almost accusingly.

I step forward and finger the edge of the paper. It is a charcoal sketch of my upper body, and the look upon my face is one of anger; it is precisely, disconcertingly, the look I must have worn when I climbed the stairs only moments ago. The eyes are dark and opened wide with anger, the mouth is closed, lips pressed tightly together, and the brows are knit together in a furrowed frown. But what strikes me most about the woman in the portrait, much more than her apparent state of high emotion, is her beauty. For despite my expression, he has made me striking. And although the face is undoubtedly my own, the beauty I do not recognise. I have never seen myself in such a light; nor has anyone else, to my knowledge. I stare at the sketch, wondering what exactly he has done to render such a transformation, which parts of me he has altered to my benefit. Slowly I turn round and find my reflection in the great gilded mirror which hangs opposite where I stand. And there, framed in the glass, is the woman of the portrait. I stand watching her, eyes wide, and the anger falls away from me like sheets of ice. I edge closer to the mirror, peer intently at myself, for I have never met the woman that he sees.

After several moments, I tear my eyes from hers, and turn back to the table. I lift the drawing in my fingers, only to discover another one below it. This, too, is me, but it is an earlier version, one I recognise more easily: the dress I wore the first day I sat with him in my master's library, the day I spoke for hours while he listened and sketched idly. This time I am not angry, but nervous and intent. And while the portrait is not unflattering, it does not hold the beauty of the first.

Slowly I lift the sheet to reveal a third, and this one takes my breath away, for in it I lie sleeping. My hair is fanned across the pillow, and one arm curls idly round my head in a gesture that is almost wanton. My lips are parted slightly and my eyes appear just closed, as if any second I will wake. My heart races as I stare at the sketch, for it is obvious that it was not imagined. He must have been there in my room, watching while I slept. And once again, the woman he has drawn is both starkly beautiful, and strikingly feminine. I feel my mouth grow dry and my face grow hot, but while I should feel anger at what is obviously a transgression on his part, I feel only confusion, as if the world around me has suddenly been shaken by an unseen hand.

There are two more sketches in the pile, both roughly rendered, as if they had been done hurriedly. One is of me in the alehouse, drawn from across the room from his place by the fire: a hasty sketch of my profile as I stand at the bar. The other is more difficult to place, for I am outside and it has been drawn at a greater distance than the others. There are trees behind me and I stand staring down at the earth. In a flash it comes to me, for I am at *her* graveside, the night her body was taken. He has drawn no one else who was present on that occasion, neither Long Boy nor Samuell nor Mary. It is only me, standing in the moonlight by her grave.

I replace the pictures and let myself out of his room, leaving the door ajar just as I had found it. I am stunned by the sketches, feel as if there is another part of me that dwells somewhere within him. Who is this woman that he sees? Now that I have seen her I cannot put her from my mind. And as I descend the tower stairs, Cook's words float across my memory like embers in the breeze: take care he does not steal your soul.

Chapter Eighteen

M y mistress lies awake when I enter, her eyes disconcertingly wide, as if her body seeks to salvage what remains of her failing vision. She turns her head in small, trembling movements to face me, manages to nod a sort of greeting. Once again I am shocked at the speed with which her strength and vitality have ebbed, for the tide of health has indeed turned against her.

'You were here earlier?' she asks. Her tone is half demanding, half fearful.

'Yes,' I say. 'While you slept.'

She nods again, relieved.

'Would you take some food?' I ask.

She waves a hand in disgust. 'I sent for Edward,' she says. 'He has been much . . . distracted of late. This business of the painter, I suppose. My own fault really.' She looks down, appears to forget herself. After a minute, her head snaps up. 'I asked him to intervene on her behalf,' she says. 'Your mother's behalf.' I stare at her. 'He was not unwilling,' she continues. 'So you see he is not without feelings, or regard, for your person,' she adds pointedly.

'Thank you, mum,' I murmur.

'He is unused to exploiting his title. Influence does not come easily to him, in the way that it did to his father. So we shall have to see.'

I think of his father, *my* father, and the tale my mother told of the manservant he nearly flogged to death. Is this what she regards as influence? I feel suddenly as if I should not be here, that I cannot serve her in good faith any longer.

'When you and Edward have married, there will be much you have to learn. I was very young when I married, had no idea what to . . . expect.' She pauses, her eyes flit across the room towards the window. 'It was a difficult period in my life.' She turns back to me and smiles wanly. 'But I survived. And so shall you.'

I stare at her, cannot bring myself to speak. Like my mother, she survived him. And in a sense so have I, for he has altered the course of life for all of us. She begins to cough and lifts a handkerchief to her lips, discharging the contents of her mouth into it. At length the cough subsides, and she is left wracked by it, her small chest heaving from the effort.

'The two of you must marry quickly if I am to be present,' she says through a choked voice. Just then I hear a stirring in the hallway and when I turn, Edward is there in the shadows of the doorway. He clears his throat and enters, glances at me and crosses directly to her bedside.

'I've returned, Mother,' he says, taking her hand. 'I've done what you asked, but you must stop all this talk of death, for you shall be as right as rain by spring.'

My mistress looks up at him and smiles. 'She is here,' she says. 'She is waiting for you.' She waves a hand in my direction.

My master reddens and clears his throat. 'You must rest now,' he says.

'It is time now, Edward,' she continues, pressing his hand fervently.

'Please, Mother,' he says urgently, his embarrassment acute.

'I cannot wait,' she says in desperation.

He stares at her and words fail him.

'You must promise me,' she says, her voice thick with emotion.

'I cannot,' he says. There is silence then as the three of us regard each other.

'Perhaps I should go,' I say tentatively.

'No,' says Edward quickly. 'No. You must stay. For this is a *family* matter,' he says with emphasis, turning to face me. 'And you are family.'

He tells her then, the entire bloodstained tale, sparing no details. And as he does, a film of resistance seems to settle over her eyes. She does not meet my gaze even once during the telling, and her body seems to collapse upon itself, like a withered rose. My master speaks in even tones at first, but as she draws away, his voice takes on a greater urgency. When he finishes, there is a suffocating silence, and the air is heavy with her enmity. Her disbelief is almost palpable.

'She is lying.' Her voice rolls across the room to where I stand by the window, and it is thick with rancour. 'I do not know her motive,' she continues in steely tones, 'but he would not have been capable, with his weakened heart, of such an act.'

'I was there,' interjects my master. 'And I saw it. And he was not struck dead.'

'You were but a child,' she retorts.

'I saw the knife in his hand, and the blood upon the stable floor,' he says. 'I heard her screams,' he adds.

My mistress eyes him for a long moment, purses her withered lips. 'So I am to believe that he sired a bastard child without my knowledge?' she says finally.

'You can believe what you wish,' he replies wearily. 'We speak the truth.'

My mistress turns away then. 'I am tired,' she says. 'And there is pain behind my eyes. I wish to sleep.' And with that, she closes her eyes, shutting out the pain and its secrets, and the offspring of her husband.

My master slowly turns to face me, his eyes dark and his cheeks flushed with anger. The colour ebbs from his face, and with it goes something else, perhaps his pride. He bends to retrieve his walking stick and shuffles from the room without another word. I turn back to my mistress and her face is like granite, though her spindly chest rises and falls almost imperceptibly. It seems that sleep has already taken her, eased her passage from the truth.

I go below to the kitchen, seek solace from the fire in the hearth. Little George is there alone, turning spitted capon, his cheeks aflame from the heat. His eyes dart towards me with their usual mixture of curiosity and alarm. It is clear that he trusts no one on this earth, and there is little reason why he should. I look at him. His hands and brow are blackened with soot, his clothes are barely more than rags. At once I turn and walk down the passage to the larder, where I remove a handful of figs and sugared dates from a wooden barrel. I return to the kitchen, hold them out to Little George. He stares in disbelief at my open palm. His eyes widen, then just as suddenly they narrow as he gazes up at me suspiciously. I hold my palm out closer to him with the ghost of a nod, challenge him to take the offering. He glances round the room, then quickly takes the fruit, cramming half into his mouth and stowing the rest beneath his tunic.

I retreat to the other side of the table, draw up a stool and begin to peel a pile of onions Cook has left lying there. Little George sits watching me covertly, his mouth still full of dates, the turnspit momentarily forgotten. I do not know what has prompted this act of charity on my part, whether it is guilt over the wedge I have driven between my mistress and her only son, or anger over her denial of the sins committed by her husband. For though he is dead and buried, he is still the master of this house: I can feel his presence all around us, built into its very timbers.

Cook enters carrying water from the yard, and casts an unsuspecting eye over Little George, nodding approvingly at the nicely browned capon. She sets the pail of water down and crosses to where I sit.

'Anne Wycombe is without,' she says quietly, nodding towards the yard. 'She has some business with you.'

I rise at once, wiping the acrid juice of onions on a rag, and hurry out into the yard where Anne Wycombe waits, anxiously twisting her leather apron in her hands.

'What has happened?' I demand.

'He is gone,' she says. 'The Long Boy.'

'When?'

'I left him sleeping late this morning. His fever had returned, and I went to fetch water. It was not the first time I had left him,' she adds defensively. I place a hand upon her arm in reassurance. 'When I returned, he was gone. I looked for him around the village, even asked at the alehouse, but he has not been seen.'

'It may be nothing. He said he wanted to go out,' I say.

She shakes her head doubtfully. 'He has taken things from the cottage. Bedclothes, and some bread and other food. I do not think he will return before nightfall.'

'You are not to blame,' I say. 'Go home and rest. I will go to the cottage and await him. If he does not return by dark, we will notify the magistrate.'

She nods, a little hesitantly, as if she is uncertain whether to leave the matter in my hands.

'Go now,' I say a little more forcefully, and with a sudden sigh of relief, she nods obediently and hurries from the yard. I watch her back disappear down the lane. When I turn back towards the kitchen, Cook is standing in the doorway.

'There is trouble?' she asks when I enter.

'The boy has run away,' I say. She frowns and I walk past her into the kitchen, take some rolls down from the ceiling basket and stuff them in the pocket of my kirtle.

'Where would he go?' she asks.

I shake my head. 'Perhaps to find his mother,' I say.

I check the alehouse first. When I tell Samuell and Mary to keep a close eye upon the stables, Samuell frowns. 'He may wish to see her,' I explain. Mary nods and lays a hand upon Samuell's arm.

'We will watch for him,' she says.

'What news have you heard of the magistrate?' I ask.

'None this day. Your master was here this morning. They remained within for some time,' she says.

'Is the magistrate there now?' I ask.

She shakes her head. 'He asked for his horse to be brought round and said he would return by nightfall.'

I nod, relieved that he has other matters elsewhere to attend to. With him away, I need not worry about my mother.

I go to Long Boy's cottage, now deserted. Even the embers in the fire have grown cold. Anne Wycombe was right, for it is instantly apparent that the boy has taken things: the quilted cover from his trundle is missing, and when I open the larger of the trunks, I see that the woollen blankets are also gone. He has not touched his mother's bedclothes, however, and I wonder at this. Perhaps he has not gone to find her after all.

I set about building a fire, piling kindling as high as it will go, for the house is deathly cold. Anne Wycombe has indeed been conscientious in her duties, for the tiny cottage is spotless. I consider going in search of the boy, but know not where to look, so I decide that there is little else to do but wait. I have not told my mother of his disappearance, believing she has enough to worry her at the moment, and I am hopeful that he will return of his own accord. If nothing else, cold or hunger may drive him home before the night is through. The fire blazes quickly and I draw a chair up to the hearth and take a roll out of my pocket, for I have eaten nothing since yesterday. A jug of ale lies on the table and I pour myself a mug. Next to it is the painter's sketch of Long Boy, and now that I am not consumed with anger, I can see that the boy was right, for the painter has caught his very essence. It is the eyes which define him: remote, uneasy, disturbed.

I do not know what motivates the painter, whether it is curiosity or some form of opportunism. Or perhaps he is in search of something different altogether, for it occurs to me that he is a man without a place. Like Dora he has left behind his people and his homeland and now surrounds himself with strangers, defined only by his talent.

As I stare into the fire, I hear footsteps on the threshold. The door pushes open slowly to reveal the painter standing there. He steps inside, and stands silently regarding me. There is a look of melancholy in his eyes which I have never seen before. He removes his hat and takes a few steps into the room, glancing towards the bare trundle in the corner.

'Where is the boy?' he asks.

'He has disappeared,' I answer.

'When?'

'This afternoon.'

His eyes drift downwards to the sketch on the table.

'It is a good likeness,' I tell him.

'At least I have accomplished that much,' he says with a wan smile. I think of the others in his room, the ones of me. Are they also his accomplishments? The painter stares down at the sketch again.

'The boy was restless,' he says, looking up at me. 'He told me that his mother ran away.'

'Maybe that is how he sees her death.'

'He said that she no longer wanted him. Perhaps all children feel this when their parents die,' he adds, turning away.

I look at him, remember that he, too, was left an orphan at the same age. 'Did you?' I ask.

He considers this for a moment. 'I felt my place was with them,' he says finally.

'And where is it now?' I ask.

'I do not know,' he says slowly, and for the first time I catch a glimpse of his uncertainty. He has done this deliberately, allowed me to see this, but I do not know why.

'Why did you come here?' I ask finally.

'To return these.' He removes the diary and the miniature from his pouch and holds them out to me, as if they are an offering of peace. I hesitate before accepting them, for suddenly I do not want the responsibility that they bring. The burden of it all seems too great: the boy's disappearance, my mother's incarceration, the desecration of Dora's corpse. I finger the crimson diary.

'Did you read it?' I ask.

He nods. 'I had to know if it was hers,' he says, his tone embarrassed.

'And?'

He shakes his head. 'It was written by her mother.'

I feel a stab of disappointment as she slips once again from our grasp.

'What did you hope to find?' I ask.

'She left me with so many questions. I thought perhaps there'd be some explanation . . . but it was foolish of me.'

I open the book, examine its brittle yellowed pages and the sloping scrawl of a woman now long dead. We were both foolish to think that Dora's secrets could be so easily laid bare. And yet she'd kept the diary with her all this time.

'She must have loved her mother very much,' I say.

'They could not have been more different,' the

painter murmurs. 'The woman who wrote this was consumed by fear.'

I think of my mother's words; Dora, too, had been afraid and in the end it killed her. Perhaps they weren't so different after all.

'What did she fear?' I ask.

'Her husband. According to the diary, she'd inherited a small fortune which by rights was his when she married him. But she'd contrived a means of withholding it, so that on her death it would go instead to Dora. He hated her for it and disputed Dora's birthright. He claimed she was the product of an earlier affair. But Dora greatly resembled him, especially in her size, so it was plain enough to see that she was his, a fact which infuriated him even more. Towards the end he threatened to kill them both.'

'What happened?'

'Her mother eventually fell ill from the strain. She writes that she would rather surrender herself to the arms of God than remain within her husband's house. Dora pleaded with her to flee the country, but she refused, saying she had not the strength or the courage to defy him.'

'But Dora did,' I say.

'Yes.'

'Did she kill him?'

'I do not know. She told me once that her parents never should have come together on this earth, and that the proof of this was lodged somewhere deep inside her.'

'What did she mean?'

He shakes his head. 'She refused to explain.'

I think of Dora and her peculiar blend of brawn and grace, almost as if her parents fought to preserve themselves through her very flesh and blood.

'I felt . . . almost a sense of shame when I read it,' says the painter quietly. 'All these years I have struggled to find the truth in people's faces . . . but here, in these words, there is so much despair. I almost could not bear to read it.' He glances at me self-consciously. 'That does not say much for me, I suppose. For my compassion.'

I open the miniature and stare at the portrait of her mother. For the first time I see the shadow of despair behind her eyes. 'He has found it,' I say. 'The painter of this miniature.'

'He was not afraid to paint what he saw. But he loved her in spite of it.'

'Your teacher.'

He nods. 'She mentions briefly their affair some years before. Her husband learned of it and she was forced to break it off.'

'Dora must have known,' I say, thinking aloud. 'Otherwise she would not have sought his help when she fled the country. Or yours.'

The painter looks at me. 'She never asked for my help,' he says slowly. 'It was I who sought to help her.' His tone is confessional, as if he feels compelled to say this, and the past spreads out between us like a vast ocean.

I nod towards the diary. 'How does it end?'

'Abruptly. She fell ill with consumption and ceased to write. She must have died soon after. Though whether it was the illness or her husband which finally killed her, it is impossible to know.'

'Perhaps both were to blame,' I say. I think of Dora, and the money hidden beneath her floorboards, money which she took but would not use. And I remember the rumours which followed her across the sea. Perhaps she did kill him, her mother's tormentor. Or perhaps she'd only wanted to.

The painter takes a step forward in the half-light and I am suddenly aware that we are but two bodies close together in a room. It is as if someone strikes a flint within me, and the slow burn that follows banishes all thoughts of that other time. I search his face for those things which still remain hidden, for I am determined to unearth the truth. I think of his words that night on the road, his swift and chilling purposefulness.

'You lied to me that night on the road,' I say. 'The commission was not your only interest.'

His expression softens, but he does not offer any defence.

'I found the sketches in your room,' I continue.

'I left them there for you to see,' he answers.

'Why?'

'So you would know,' he says. 'It was not *her* I wanted.'

Slowly the breath escapes me. I look down at my hands. It is this he wants: my flesh, my body, my bones.

He takes another step forward and I slowly raise my eyes to look at him. And then I feel her presence all around us, for we are in *her* house, and she is compelling me to finish what we started.

The painter stops in front of me, looks at me intently. 'What is it?' he asks.

I stare at him, and her unseen presence envelops me like a mist. 'She is here with us,' I say.

He shakes his head. 'She is dead.'

My eyes travel around the room, searching for some confirmation of this fact, but my uneasiness persists. 'I am afraid.'

He meets my gaze. 'It is not her you fear, but yourself.' Then he extends his hand towards mine, and I place my fingers in his. It is a simple gesture, but it feels as if we hold the heat of the earth within our hands. He draws me gently towards him, and the fear falls away, leaving only a deep current of desire. I find his lips then, search for their taste and warmth and softness. I feel his hands encircle my waist, glide beneath the fabric of my dress, caress my skin. The muscles deep within me tighten. Our bodies press together and I pull him back onto her bed, burn to feel his weight on me.

The painter's hands move quickly, tearing at the laces and the whalebones and the stays, endeavouring to find an entrance to the bone house that is me. I push myself against him, rub my flesh into his, cannot merge our bodies as tightly as I wish. And despite his words, I feel her there within me, urging me on. For in her bed my transformation is complete; in that moment he possesses both of us, myself and Dora, buried somewhere deep inside me.

Perhaps in spirit I am not my mother's child after all, but the daughter of the great-bellied woman, she who follows only rules of her own making.

Afterwards, we lie together.

'What will you do now?' I ask.

'I do not know.'

'Will you finish her portrait?'

'No,' he says. 'Your mother was right.' I smile at this: the two of them in unlikely accord. 'I have no other commission,' he continues, his voice trailing off. There is an awkward silence, as we both contemplate the meaning of this.

'I had thought to make a journey when my work here was complete,' he says tentatively.

'You are fortunate to have such liberty,' I reply. I feel both disappointment and envy at his words, and turn away from him to conceal my dismay. Slowly I rise and begin to pull on my serving woman's clothes: the clothes that bind me to the Great House and its secrets.

The painter raises himself up on one elbow. 'I have no wish to drift forever,' he says earnestly. 'But I've not yet found a place where I belong.'

I stop dressing and turn to him. His naked chest glistens in the light of the taper.

'Perhaps it is not a place you seek, but a person.'

He looks at me and I feel the heat rise in my face. I turn and pick up his tunic, and as I do the miniature tumbles from the bedclothes and drops to the floor. I stoop to retrieve it and see at once that the glass has shattered: a neat web of lines now encases her. I glance up at him anxiously; I feel that we have transgressed her. The painter reaches over and gingerly closes the frame, protecting her from further danger.

'It will be safe in the chest,' he says.

I cross the room and lift the chest onto the table. I feel for the secret latch along the side, and once again, as if by magic, the top springs open. And there beneath the lid I find the answer to our questions, for the swaddling clothes have disappeared.

And all at once I know where I will find the boy.

We finish dressing quickly, the painter eyeing me curiously when I tell him we must hurry. I grab my cloak and he follows me outside, just as dusk begins to close in upon us. Without thinking I take his hand, pull him along through the forest behind her cottage, along a path just barely visible through the trees. We do not speak and there is little noise other than the sound of our feet upon the frozen snow.

At length the path disappears but we continue through the forest. Once or twice I pause to check my bearings, for I have not been this way since I was a child, but memory and instinct guide me like an unseen beacon. The painter looks back anxiously once or twice, for night is falling, and we have brought nothing to light our safe return.

As the last rays of daylight disappear, we reach the stream where Dora died. The moon is nearly full and casts an eerie light upon us, reflecting off the snow. We move along the icy stream bed, slowly picking our way through rocks and twisted roots and frozen mud, tracing its serpentine course for some minutes. At length the walls of the bed begin to climb more steeply, until we find ourselves within a deep ravine, bounded on all sides by lichen-covered granite. I stop and hold a hand up to the painter, pointing across the stream to a series of sheer rock walls which rise steeply from the bed. Further along, a few of them have openings, great fissures where the force of nature has split the rock asunder.

We stand staring up at it, our breath forming icy jets of fog that vanish almost instantly in the cold night air. The painter stoops down, cupping water from the stream in his hands, and drinks deeply of it. At length he rises, wiping his hands on his tunic.

'What is this place?' he says in a hushed voice.

I point towards the ravine.

'This is where they found her body,' I explain. 'Up there, in the caves along the rock face. I used to come here in the summer as a child. In my day it was a secret place. But now the village children all come here to play.'

The painter looks around in wonder, for it is hauntingly beautiful.

'It is a magical place,' I say. 'A place for children.'

He turns to me then, divines my meaning. 'The boy is here?' he says, his eyes wide.

I nod and raise a finger to my lips. I motion him to follow and slowly, quietly, we move along the stream bed, choosing a narrow place where we can ford the icy water, picking our way across the stones. When we reach the base of the rock wall, I stop and stare up at the caves. Something catches my eye in the largest, a movement, and I point to it and begin to climb along the giant plates of stone. The moss has made it treacherous, twice I slip, and the painter raises a hand from behind to prevent my fall. Eventually we find a crack which is deep enough to move along, and we cross it carefully, mindful of the drop beneath us.

As we reach the largest opening, we pull ourselves inside, stooping to avoid the ceiling. It takes only a few seconds for my eyes to adjust to the darkness within, and there, crouched in the furthest reach, is the shivering figure of the boy. He holds a bundle closely to his chest, a tightly wrapped blanket, one of those from the trunk, and watches us, wild-eyed. I take a step forward, instinctively hold out a hand.

'Long Boy, you are cold,' I say. He shifts sideways like a crab in an effort to retreat. But there is nowhere for him to go. I take another step, crouch down, my fingers resting lightly on the damp stone.

'You must come home,' I say gently. 'You cannot stay the night here.'

'Do not take him from me,' he says urgently.

I stare at the bundle. 'He needs warmth,' I say. 'He belongs with his mother. She will warm him.'

Long Boy eyes me distrustfully, shakes his head. 'He is mine,' he says.

'We will bring him with us then,' I say coaxingly. 'My mother waits for you. For both of you.'

He considers my words, and as he does I ease myself forward. I pause just in front of him and hold my arms out for the bundle. He stares down at my hands. Slowly I take the bundle from him, feel its stiffness. He does not resist. I cradle the bundle in my arms, peel back the frozen blanket.

The baby is immaculate in its woollen tomb. Its features are tiny and perfectly formed, and its arms are pulled up, fists frozen tightly against its chest. Long Boy must have wiped the blood away, for its skin is flat and white like just-made pastry. I pull the blanket away to reveal the sex: a baby boy. Long Boy stares at the dead child in my arms.

'We will take the baby with us,' I say. 'And return him to your mother.'

Long Boy raises his head to look at me, his eyes filled with pain. 'She would not have me,' he says searchingly. 'She would have the others. But not me.' Long Boy looks once more at the tiny infant and swallows. I hold my breath, glance behind me to the painter, who raises his eyebrows. I turn back to the boy.

'Long Boy, did you push her?' I ask gently.

He continues staring at the infant, his chest heaving from the memory.

'She ran from me,' he says. 'She ran and ran . . . and then she fell.' He looks up at me, tears in his eyes. 'She did not want me any more.'

And then his meaning dawns on me, for in my arms I hold the devil's child, and it is both his brother and his son.

The painter gathers up the bedclothes and the remaining food and, with me still carrying the infant, we begin our descent. Long Boy follows soundlessly behind us. Slowly we edge our way back along the crevice in the rock wall, with the painter in the lead and Long Boy bringing up the rear, his face impassive, as if in a trance. As we near the bottom I pause and look back. He has stopped several yards behind. He turns and begins climbing back towards the cave and I call to him, but he is moving swiftly, purposefully, and does not respond. The painter, too, pauses and we exchange a worried glance. Perhaps Long Boy has forgotten something, though the cave appeared empty when we left it.

He reaches the opening and does not stop, but continues past it, clambering along the crack in the rock face. It narrows until it provides barely more than a handhold, but he moves easily, hauling his giant frame across the wall of rock like an oversized insect. The rock rises another twenty feet above the level of the cave entrance, and we watch helplessly as he reaches the top and hauls himself up over the edge, disappearing from view.

I shout his name, and my cries bounce against the sheer rock, mocking me. We wait in silence for a moment, hoping he will reappear, knowing that it is pointless to follow. Even if we were to find him, he is far too strong for us to restrain. We wait in silence, can hear nothing now but the trickle of the stream below, and the deathly silence of the forest.

And then he reappears on top of the ridge some distance downstream, where the rock reaches its highest point, perhaps a hundred feet above the stream bed. He moves forward to the edge of the cliff and I watch in knowing horror as he contemplates the water far below. I call to him one last time and he does not appear to hear, does not even glance in our direction. And then I see him raise his arms and cast himself forward, as if he is a giant bird, soaring down across the rock face, plummeting towards his mother far below.

He lands face down on a bed of jagged rocks which line the water's edge, and we watch in horror as his blood slowly mingles with the icy water of the stream. The painter edges back towards me, reaches out a hand and pulls me to him, for I stand frozen, unable to tear my eyes from Long Boy's lifeless body. I clutch the infant tightly to my chest, as if by doing so I can still preserve its life. But they are all dead now, the mother and her sons, and there is nothing I can do.

Later, I sit upon the bank and watch as the painter drags Long Boy's body from the rocks onto the snowy shore, laying him face down. I no longer notice the cold, feel only the weight of the tiny child in my arms. Somehow she must have known it was the boy's. I can only wonder what must have gone between them: the mother with the body of a thousand women, the child with that of a fully-grown man.

Chapter Nineteen

We leave him there face down upon the icy bank and return to the village with the dead child still locked in my arms. This time it is the painter who leads me through the forest, for I have no more consciousness than a sleepwalker. He takes me straight to the alehouse, and I stand by the kitchen fire unable to speak while Mary gently prises the infant from my grasp. The painter then knocks upon the magistrate's door, and spills forth the story of the boy and his mother and the terrible fate that claimed them both.

I wait by the fire while they speak, a tankard of untouched ale between my palms, and Mary by my side. Try as I might, I cannot banish the image of the boy in flight from my mind, his arms spread wide to catch the earth.

At length the painter reappears, his face grim but relieved. He kneels in front of me and takes the tankard from my hands, presses his palms against my own. I look into his eyes, try to lose myself in them, and feel an overwhelming tiredness, as if I have lived a lifetime in the course of a day. He draws me slowly to my feet, urging me to return with him to the Great House. But I shake my head and silence him, for there is something I must do.

Together we walk to my mother's cottage, and at her door I leave him, insisting that he return alone to the Great House. When he is gone, I enter quietly and find her dozing in a chair beside the fire, her fingers clutching a skein of half-wound wool. A low-burning taper flickers in an iron holder upon the table, casting a muted circle of light round it. My mother does not wake when I enter, and I stand for a moment watching her while she sleeps, her head lolling gently to one side.

She is no longer the woman who inhabits my childhood memories, but another person altogether: a woman who is privy to dark secrets, and one who has been preyed upon by her own people. Such things come to bear upon a person, make their mark, and she will carry it with her always, just as I will. I look for it now in the line of her sagging jaw or the fleshy folds of her neck, or the wrinkles upon the backs of her hands. Her life has held much toil and sadness. And yet I have no doubt that when she wakes she will not harbour bitterness against her accusers, for it is not in her nature to dwell upon the past, any more than it is to dream of the future. She is like the river salmon bent upon its homecoming: she will only seek to repossess her former life.

I lay a hand gently upon her shoulder and she

wakens with a start. 'It is only me,' I say softly. Her eyes drift over to the taper.

'I did not mean to sleep,' she says, drawing herself up in the chair. I pull a stool across to face her and seat myself, not quite sure how to begin.

'The boy is dead,' I say finally, starting at the end. And then I tell the tale in its entirety, while she listens, close-lipped, her knuckles white against the chair. When I am finished she gives an enormous sigh and we both turn our faces to the dying embers of the fire. I sense no malice from her, no trace of blame as I had feared, and for that I am grateful. Indeed she appears more calm than I have seen her in some days, as if the truth has stilled her.

'Did you know of this?' I ask her finally.

She looks at me and shakes her head. 'No.' She gives another sigh. 'Perhaps a part of me knew.' She squints at the memory. 'She wanted me to understand. She gave me clues. Towards the end, there was a great longing in her to relive the past, to undo what she had done. She needed to atone . . . but most of all she needed sympathy . . . and absolution.' My mother looks at me. 'The latter was not mine to give.' Her voice trails off in sadness. 'The day before she died, she told me that she had not chosen fate, but rather had created it. I did not understand her meaning until now. I told her that our fate was in God's hands. And she said that his judgement had been harsh and terrible.' My mother looks at me. 'As always, she was right.' We sit in silence for a moment.

'I am sorry about the boy,' I say finally.

'I thought that I could save him from her sins,' replies my mother. 'But I did not know that they were *his* sins too. They are both in God's hands now.'

'We have been to see the magistrate,' I say. 'You are free now.'

She nods, frowning into the flames. 'It will be hard to carry on without them,' she says. 'At least with the boy, I had a piece of her.'

I reach for her hand and take it in mine, a gesture only Dora's death has allowed me. I think of my master and my mother, and the private battles they will have to wage before they are set free. For grief is like a mountain to be climbed: only from its highest point can we see beyond.

I leave her staring into the fire, her hands newly tangled in the wool. Even my mother is not alone, for we are all strung together in our longing.

When I reach the Great House it is late, but I do not climb the stairs to my tiny chamber; I go instead to the tower. As I pass the library, a feeble light shows beneath the door, a sign that my master remains restless within. I glide past his door without a sound until I reach the painter's chamber, which I enter without knocking, surprised at my own boldness. He is reading in bed and looks up when I enter, his eyes anxious in the half-light of the candle beside him. I lock the door and move across the room without a word, and he closes the book and moves over in his bed. I lie down next to him, place my head upon his chest, and close my eyes to all that I have seen and heard. The painter strokes my hair for a moment, then leans over and extinguishes the candle, and before I know it sleep has taken me.

I wake in the light of pre-dawn, still fully clothed, my back aching from the rigours of my corset. The painter sleeps and I take care not to disturb him as I rise. I need to undress, to release my body from its cage of whalebone stays and cotton ties, even if only for a few minutes, so I steal out of the room and return to the privacy of my bedchamber where I quickly remove everything and slip beneath the bed-clothes, shivering in the morning cold. I close my eyes and once again fall into sleep, but though my bed is empty I am not alone.

She comes to me in my dreams, and this time she is no longer troubled but strangely calm. She stands in the cave entrance, her white dress billowing in the wind, and there is an air of poignant resignation about her, as if the worst has happened and been overcome. I call to her from down below and slowly her eyes swivel round to find me. I try to scramble up the crevice in the rock but my hands and feet cannot find their hold, and when I look again she has disappeared from view. I stand there searching the cave openings, desperate for one last glimpse of her, and after a moment she reappears on top of the ridge in the same spot where the boy jumped to his death. This time Long Boy is at her side, nearly a head taller than she is but clutching her hand boyishly like the man-child he is. I raise my arm to wave at them but this time she does not respond, does not even look in my direction. They stand there together for several moments, and then she turns and leads him away from the cliff edge, away for ever from my view. I turn and look along the stream bed to the spot where Long Boy landed and his body is still there, face down upon the bank, but I know that it is empty, for his soul has flown.

And then I look at my hands, and they are not my own but hers: large and strong and scratched and bloody from the fall that claimed her. I stare at them, wonder whether she has bequeathed them to me, and if so, what purpose they will serve. And in the next instant they are gone, for suddenly I am wide awake, looking out upon the cold light of winter in my chamber.

It is only a matter of hours before news of Long Boy's death spreads through the village, as do the details of the events which preceded it. A group of men retrieve his body during the course of the morning, and by dusk he has been laid to rest alongside his mother in the graveyard, the boy infant in her arms. We all attend the burial, just as we had done not ten days earlier, but so much has happened in the interim that there is little to recall that earlier scene. My mother draws a few glances from the villagers, but by and large they keep their tongues and their wits about them. And when the burial is over, my master shuffles slowly across the frozen earth and clasps my mother's hand in both of his, a gesture which surprises both of them. Only my mistress is conspicuous by her absence, for she lies dying in her bed.

She has refused to speak to me since yesterday, and waits patiently, almost longingly, for death to claim her. When I went to see her in the morning, she closed her eyes and turned her face away, a gesture of repudiation which, oddly, left me unmoved. Perhaps she simply acknowledges with her actions what we both know to be true: that the ground has shifted beneath our feet, and nothing remains as it was.

For once, the people of the village are struck dumb by the truth. Though many are horrified by Long Boy's crimes, he was her son, and she was almost sacred to them. When the burial is over they purse their lips, draw their cloaks more tightly round their shoulders, and slowly return to the numbing silence of their work.

After the burial I accompany my mother to Dora's cottage, to claim those things that were most precious to her: the wooden chest and its contents, including the tiny shattered portrait of her mother and the diary filled with words she will never understand. I hesitate when my eyes come to rest on the spot where her money lies buried. I cannot bring myself to unearth it now, but know that it is there – that it may one day purchase opportunity. The painter waits patiently outside while we go through her possessions, and when we emerge, my mother clutching the wooden box tightly to her chest, the two of them come face to face. She hesitates, then nods at him and he falls in beside us, and together we return to her house, just as night begins to fall. We leave her there, the painter and I, and she does not seem to question his presence any longer, merely thanks us for our help and bids us goodnight.

Together we walk slowly back to the Great House, pausing at the graveyard one last time. I stare at the freshly mounded earth which covers them, knowing that they are somewhere else, on top of the ridge, far away. The painter takes my shoulders in his hands and turns me slowly round to face him.

'Come with me across the water,' he says.

My eyes flicker back to her grave. I think of her flight and the world she left behind, the world of the diary. At once I see my own life on its yellowed pages: the years of loneliness and servitude, of visions and nightmares. Like her I long for more, but I do not wish my flight to end as hers has done.

The painter looks at me and reads my thoughts. 'We cannot know our end,' he says.

I nod, knowing he is right, look down at my hands and this time see my own flesh and bones. If not her hands, then what has she bequeathed me? I close my eyes and struggle to see her, cannot find her features in the darkness of my mind.

But instinct tells me she is there, somewhere deep inside me, and that she will set me free.